Bullets slammed against the side of the snowmobile

Bolan felt one round bite deep below his left knee, then he had the M-16 up and tracking the small knot of men confronting him. He sprayed a long burst from left to right as he roared toward them. Three gunners dived away in headlong plunges, losing their weapons.

The silvery flash of a Lear jet on the runway caught the warrior's attention. A Jeep shrieked to a stop near the hangar, and the Executioner recognized Konrad Dreyse as the man swung out of the driver's seat.

The view was suddenly blocked by a two-ton truck that swung in front of Bolan, the driver's face grim as he bore down on the warrior's Arctic Cat. Short bursts ate into the cowling of the snowmobile.

Trapped, with no time and no room to maneuver, Bolan watched the chain-covered tires sweep toward him.

MACK BOLAN®

The Executioner

DON PENDLETON'S
THE EXECUTIONER®
FEATURING MACK BOLAN®

NIGHT HIT

A GOLD EAGLE BOOK FROM
WORLDWIDE®

TORONTO • NEW YORK • LONDON • PARIS
AMSTERDAM • STOCKHOLM • HAMBURG
ATHENS • MILAN • TOKYO • SYDNEY

First edition October 1991

ISBN 0-373-61154-4

Special thanks and acknowledgment to
Mel Odom for his contribution to this work.

NIGHT HIT

Injustice anywhere is a threat to justice everywhere.
—Martin Luther King, Jr.
August 1963

Justice is something I believe in. That belief has been sorely tried from time to time, but I cling to it. And if the pursuit of justice transcends state or international boundaries, and if I have to help it along, I never hesitate. I never will.
—Mack Bolan

To the dedicated Armed Forces of
the United States of America

PROLOGUE

A cold, black wind blew death into Chicago.

Karl Moltke sat quietly in the passenger seat of the Volkswagen van. He allowed no smoking, and he allowed no idling of the van's engine to warm his men.

"How long has it been?" he asked the driver in German.

"Eighteen minutes," Hollmann responded quickly in the same language.

Moltke nodded and shifted on the seat, moving the large trench coat over his weapons, keeping them covered. Every so often a late-night shopper would wander by, hunkered over against the biting wind. It wouldn't do to alarm any of them by allowing a glance at the H&K 9 mm pistol sheathed across the body armor covering his chest, or the pump-action Mossberg 590 at his side.

The Chicago Police Department would be on the alert for robbers. After all, this was the Christmas season. Moltke didn't want to be confused for a two-bit thief.

Five minutes more passed.

Moltke reached for the door and popped it open. The six men in the back shuffled into movement. "Hollmann, stay with the vehicle. You three—" he pointed quickly, using a gloved forefinger "—come with me. The others I want in a scattered perimeter around the van. You are to maintain radio silence until I break it.'' He stared into their eyes, making sure they knew there would be no excuses.

Fisting the Mossberg under the gray trench coat, Moltke took a straight approach toward Lake Michigan, fanning the others out behind him with a wave.

From the side road where the van had been left, off South Lake Shore Drive, it was only a matter of minutes to the yacht basin where their assigned target was. For a few seconds, he allowed his mind to dawdle with the possibilities of what had gone wrong with the mission, then he banished the thoughts and let his military instincts come back into play.

He went silently down the dock, knowing the three other members of his team had taken up positions behind him and would be covering him with the sniping rifles they carried. A young couple addressed him in English as he moved toward the vessel he was interested in. He responded in kind, flashing a smile, and went on.

He passed the *Vanessa,* running a critical eye along the 52-foot yacht, the hobbyist-sailor in him appreciating what he saw. Then he was beyond it, moving for the vessel one slip farther. There were no lights visible in this craft. His feet made no noise as he gained the deck, nor as he drew the shadow around him and used it to see him safely to the other side.

Kneeling, he freed the Mossberg and placed it beside him. The yacht listed in the dark waters. He adjusted for it as he drew the pocket binoculars to his eyes and peered into the cabin.

Moltke saw Klaus first, saw the blood staining the young man's forehead as he kept his hands behind his

neck and his face on the floor. Nohles lay in a crumpled heap beside Klaus, unmoving. Taking time,
Moltke studied Nohles's throat, discovering the man
was still alive.

A young woman dressed in a lavender bathrobe
talked excitedly into the phone she held. Her hands
shook, and she kept pushing her short, blond hair
from her face. The man holding the gun on Klaus appeared to be in more control of himself. He held the
gun in both hands, in a professional manner.

Moltke put the binoculars away, then, shotgun in
hand, made his way to the stern of his ship. Easing
into the small rowboat tied up beside the yacht, he
slipped the oars into the water and rowed for the *Vanessa*.

Keeping the small boat from hitting the yacht,
Moltke slithered up the side of the craft, placing his
additional weight slowly and carefully, grateful the
cold winds kept the surface choppy. He slipped the
safety off the Mossberg as he knelt beside the window.

The young woman was still on the phone, still talking emotionally to whoever was on the other end.

A police siren howled in the distance as Moltke took
a step and slid into position, holding the pistol grip of
the pump shotgun tightly.

The man maintaining the two-handed grip on the
.357 tried to wheel and bring his weapon to bear, a
premature shot ripping through the carpet at Klaus's
knees. The thunderous crack of the heavy-caliber pistol startled the woman into dropping the phone.

Without hesitation, Moltke triggered a round of 12-
gauge solid shot into the man's bare chest, racking the

slide, then following immediately with another round that pinned the body against the wall.

"Get the woman," Moltke ordered in German as he glanced at the few lights starting to wink on in the other yachts and houseboats.

Klaus and Nohles responded to his voice at once, pursuing and trapping the woman like a team of trained Dobermans. A glance back at the scene inside the yacht showed him the woman wasn't wearing clothing. She looked elegant, with the kind of aloofness that could drive a man crazy. He had no doubt of what had taken Klaus's and Nohles's minds off their target, and there had been no mention of a boyfriend in the files his team had been given.

"Get a coat on her," Moltke said as he stood up and started forward. The woman's screams shattered the night. He poked his head back down at the shattered window. "And a gag."

Moltke lifted a walkie-talkie from his pocket and thumbed it. "We're coming out," he said in German. "First Nohles and Klaus with the woman, and me bringing up the rear."

A few seconds later, Klaus and Nohles dragged the struggling woman up on the dock between them. Her gag appeared to be tight, and her face was white with fear. Moltke waved them on, trotting after them with the Mossberg at the ready.

At the top of the stairs leading to the main work area of the dock, a police car skidded into view, the red cherries whirling madly.

Moltke went to work, letting the recoil of the Mossberg become part of him. The shotgun belched a thunderous roll as solid shot rattled and sparked from the prowl car's front end. The first three shots put out the headlights and slammed a huge hole in the radiator. The last four shattered the windshield as the men inside tried too late to dive for cover. He used the H&K from the chest holster to finish the job the 12-gauge had started.

As he reach for more shells to reload the Mossberg, another prowl car roared onto the scene from the other end of the dock and skidded to a stop facing him. Moltke lowered the shotgun as if giving himself up, knowing his men could see him clearly in the glow of the prowl car's lights.

"Police!" one of the men shouted as the doors came open at the same time, and both officers took shelter behind them. "Hold it right—"

Then a sudden hail of bullets ripped through the glass and metal of the car, sending their corpses to litter the new-fallen snow. Neither man had gotten off a single shot.

Retrieving his weapon, Moltke continued reloading as he ran to catch up with Nohles and Klaus. He paused once he reached the shadows again, motioning his team back to the waiting van. He studied the prowl cars, watching the red glare ebb and flow over the whiteness of the snow. Even if the authorities figured out what was happening from the destruction left at the pier, the team already had more than enough hostages to make their play.

He tightened his grip on his weapon, then turned and left the scene. Either way, they'd come to savage the city, to unleash fears and take whatever money they could wring out of the citizens. Dreyse wouldn't turn back once the die had been cast. And it had. In spades.

1

"Mr. Belasko, we're on our final approach to Dulles," the pilot of the Lear jet announced over the cabin speaker. "If you're not belted up, sir, now's the time."

Bolan blinked his eyes to clear his head of the fragmented nightmares his unconscious mind had been chasing. Images of the carnage he'd seen in San Francisco and Dallas had refused to dissipate. He tested the seat belt still fastened around his waist, satisfying himself everything was still in place.

Clamping on the headset that connected him with the pilot's cabin, Bolan asked, "Have you heard from Brognola?"

"Yes, sir. Entered radio contact with him about ten minutes ago. He told me you'd be sleeping if you could, and didn't want me to patch him through. Said he could start your briefing when he came aboard."

"Right."

The Lear took up its final approach, rocking slightly as it was buffeted by crosswinds.

"Gonna be a bit bumpy," the pilot advised. Then the wheels touched with a bounce, touched again, then maintained the contact.

After the jet came to a standstill, Bolan released the seat belt and stood, stretching kinked muscles, feeling the pull of old injuries. The webbing holding the Desert Eagle and the ammo pouches was in the seat next to his, but he wore the Beretta in its shoulder holster. Even in an operation like this, with Brognola personally riding shotgun on the timetable, the Executioner never knew safe ground. The arm's-length alliance he had with the government through Justice was usually a tenuous thing at most, and generally worked in his favor only under the best of conditions.

The Lear held eight seats with a narrow walkway between the two double rows on each side. Bolan kept the interior dark despite the curtains covering the windows. Thoughts of Chicago and the savagery going down there were uppermost in his mind.

The small oval door separating the pilot's cabin from the passenger area opened, and a man in shirt and tie stepped through. The name badge hanging from his left pocket identified him as Captain Wayne Travis. He was tall and thin, with neatly cropped brown hair graying at the temples, and a gunslinger mustache that drooped dramatically on either side of his mouth.

The pilot extended a hand and Bolan took it.

"Didn't get to meet you at Miami," Travis said. He held up a red thermos. "Or offer you a cup of coffee."

"Thanks." Bolan accepted the container, hoping the brew was strong and black.

Travis went to the door and opened it, letting down the stairway. "I'm going to grab a quick bite inside while they top the tanks off. That'll give you and Brognola a little time to talk private. Can I get you anything?"

Bolan shook his head.

A dark sedan rolled up to the ramp as Travis faded into the blackness settling over the airport. Brognola got out of the sedan, caught for a moment in the headlights of the refueling truck trundling toward the Lear. The Fed had a stack of file folders under one arm that threatened to flutter away.

Bolan went down to meet him.

"Equipment cases are in the trunk," Brognola said, dropping car keys into the warrior's palm.

The cases were large and bulky, vinyl-covered with Department of Justice insignia on all sides. When the warrior hefted the first two, he found them as heavy as he knew they would be. Brognola helped on the return trip, finishing the last of the seven cases.

The equipment cases filled most of the seats on the right in the Lear. Bolan reeled up the stairway and locked the door, then used the key Brognola gave him to open the first case.

The top lifted and revealed a Belgian-made Fabrique Nationale rifle in a mat black finish outfitted with a sling and a Zeiss Diavari D telescopic sight. Boxes of 7.62 mm ammunition filled lower compartments. Satisfied, he closed the lid and moved on.

The next case contained a Franchi SPAS 15 with a folding stock. Boxes of 12-gauge shells, both solid shot and double-aught, occupied space below it. Under that was a Franchi PA3/215 pump-action shotgun that could be easily hidden under street clothing once the stock was removed. He relocked the case.

"How bad is Chicago?" Bolan asked as he opened the next case. It was small and compact compared to the first two. Inside was a Smith & Wesson Portable

Riot Control Emergency Kit, complete with 37 mm gas gun, six long-range 37 mm projectiles, six short-range 37 mm shells and four continuous discharge grenades in an equal mix of CN and CS gas.

"They've got officers down at the scene of one kidnapping," Brognola said.

"Civilians?"

"One so far, but the Chicago PD and special task-force people are expecting the body count to start climbing at any time."

Bolan closed the case. "How are they wanting to handle it?"

"They want to get their people home safe."

"Do you think that'll happen?"

"No. Neither does the Man. That's why we wanted you in on this."

Bolan nodded. "Once I'm in, Hal, there's going to be no turning back. I want you to understand that from the start. These bastards have had their way so far, but their roll stops here, with me."

"We'll give you the support we can, but we don't even know who these sons of bitches are. In both previous cities, they've been like ghosts, fading in through the night, following a series of planned strikes that leave dead scattered in their wake like so much cordwood. They figure on the major banks being open by nine the next morning. By nine-fifteen, these people are history."

"What time are we set to arrive in Chicago?"

"It's a straight shot from here," Brognola replied, pushing back a sleeve to check his watch. "We'll touch down at twelve-thirty, quarter to one their time." He adjusted his watch.

Bolan did the same. "That gives us eight hours to move on this."

Brognola gave him a tight nod. "It's more than San Francisco or Dallas got."

"Yeah." He moved on to the next case, clicking it open to reveal the Second Chance Hardcorps III body armor inside. The three frontal inserts and optional back-guard insert lay underneath. They would almost triple the armor's weight, but they also provided protection from armor-piercing rounds. He resealed the case.

"Chicago PD uses Second Chance gear," Brognola said. "It'll help keep you from getting a lot of attention from the locals for a while." He paused. "Maybe."

Bolan nodded, finished his inspection of the rest of the cases, and turned to face his friend. "What kind of intel do you have on these people?"

"Not much." Brognola sighed and picked up the first file. "Aaron's digging, but there's not a lot to go on. I can tell you more about the body count in those cities than I can about the men behind the operation. How much do you know already?"

"I was there for the aftermath of Dallas."

"You saw it?"

"Yes."

"Then you know what we're facing here." Brognola turned two of the seats down and made a makeshift table. "Take a look at these reports and let's talk."

The Executioner sat and opened the file, finding himself confronted with picture after picture of the dead in Dallas and San Francisco.

"HERE," KONRAD DREYSE said softly as he tapped his driver on the shoulder.

The driver gave a quick nod and immediately pulled the Mercedes sedan to the curb in front of the Lake Point Tower apartment building on East Illinois Street.

The back doors of the vehicle opened as the two men in the rear seat stepped out to secure the area. Cold wind, seeded with snowflakes, lashed against Dreyse's bare neck. He pulled the collar of his coat tighter.

"It's clear, colonel," Pfirsch called a moment later.

Dreyse checked the street for himself before releasing the door latch and moving toward the lobby of the skyscraper. Pfirsch and Vogelsang fell in behind him immediately, outfitted as he was in business attire and overcoat. He pushed his hands deep in the pockets, finding the twin SIG-Sauer 9 mm pistols still warm with his body heat. "Pfirsch?"

"Ja, Herr Dreyse," the man responded in his gravelly voice.

"You'll speak English as long as we're engaged in this operation."

"Yes, sir."

"Vogelsang, the doorman will be your target," Dreyse said as they approached the door. "It's imperative that he doesn't have the chance to warn anyone about us."

"Yes, sir."

Dreyse stepped to one side under the canopy overhanging the walkway, turning to look east along Illinois Street. He squinted against the falling snow and watched as a Volkswagen van pulled to a stop opposite the Mercedes. The driver switched off the lights, and the snow-filled street faded from dirty yellow back to crystalline white.

A shadow fell across the glass doors of the lobby area. Dreyse turned to smile unctuously at the uniformed doorman.

The doorman was old, his hair under the hat almost as white and lifeless as the falling snow.

Vogelsang looked almost cherubic in the security lights under the canopy. The man's face was round and smooth, looking even younger than his twenty-five years. His eyes were gray and innocent. "I forgot my key," Vogelsang said, rubbing his hands in front of him and blowing on them.

Dreyse watched the conversation with the 9 mm pistols fisted tightly. When the doorman's eyes touched his briefly, he smiled.

"Do I know you?' the doorman asked hesitantly.

Vogelsang shook his head. "I don't think so. I've never seen you. My name's Fieldhouse. Bob Fieldhouse. My uncle Mike lives on the eighteenth floor. I just flew in yesterday."

Hesitantly the doorman reached for his key.

There actually was a Michael Fieldhouse living on the eighteenth floor, just as there was a nephew. Dreyse had checked on most of the intel for these operations personally. He watched the doorman and waited.

"What suite did you say your uncle was in?" the doorman asked as he fumbled with the key.

"Eighteen-twelve," Vogelsang replied. "Like, in the war of."

Dreyse knew something had tripped the doorman's inner alarm by the way the man held his eyes, but didn't know what it could be. All of Vogelsang's intel had been carefully researched.

The doorman straightened, letting his key drop away from the lock.

"He knows," Dreyse said, motioning the men in the van into action. The doors and the side entrance opened immediately.

Vogelsang nodded, and a hard look shadowed his cherubic features as a silenced automatic materialized in his hands. The pistol coughed once, its subsonic round tunneling through the glass to catch the doorman in the throat.

Dreyse stared at the small hole in the glass with the spiderweb of cracks as Vogelsang dropped to his knees and started working on the lock. This late at night, the apartment building employed an armed security staff. Even if the team was discovered, events could still be played out as they'd been planned.

The lock snicked open and the young man slithered inside, grabbing a fistful of the doorman's uniform and dragging the body toward the men's room beside the elevator bank.

Dreyse pushed the door open with his elbow and walked inside. "Keitel, I want that window replaced now."

"Yes, sir." The man peeled away from the group to get the sheet of glass in the van that had been brought along for just such an eventuality.

"Gerlach?" Dreyse called, waving Pfirsch toward the office area.

Pfirsch went at once, his Heckler & Koch 9 mm pistol up and ready.

"Yes, sir," Gerlach responded, moving up from the back of the group.

Dreyse pointed at the blood smeared across the floor. "There are paper towels and cleansers in the men's room. See to this."

"Yes, sir." The man moved out.

Ticking the seconds off in his head, Dreyse walked toward the office area, met at the corner by Vogelsang, who bounced the doorman's keys in one hand. "The body?" the team leader asked.

"I gave Gerlach orders to secure it above the ceiling tiles."

"The blood will collect and eventually drip down," Dreyse said with a frown. "It will be a time bomb leading to discovery."

"No. I used paper towels to stuff inside the wound to stop the bleeding." He grinned thinly. "The only thing that will give the body away is the smell. By then we should be gone."

"Good."

No one appeared to be in the outer office area. The door in the back was slightly ajar.

Dreyse walked inside the outer office, taking in the array of plastic plants, glass-topped tables, moderately expensive carpet and sofas. The desk was unoccupied. "Pfirsch?" he called.

"Here," the man called from the inside office.

"Do you have the clerk?"

"Yes. It was Hanson, the big one." Pfirsch's voice sounded strained.

"Bring him out."

The door opened and Pfirsch pushed Hanson through. The night clerk was big, standing six foot four, and built like a linebacker. He towered over Pfirsch by half a head. A dark bruise was beginning to stain the clerk's temple. Pfirsch kept his pistol pointed at the back of the man's neck, the other hand holding the length of chain between the handcuffs Hanson wore.

Dreyse stared at the big man, their eyes level. "Where's Mahoney?"

"Who the hell are you guys?"

Pointing one of the SIG-Sauers between the clerk's eyes, Dreyse said, "You only get one more chance."

Hanson's eyelids twitched uncontrollably. "He called in sick. I'm covering for him."

"Till eight?"

"Yeah. The usual time."

Dreyse lowered the hammer on the pistol and put the weapon back in his pocket as he nodded toward Pfirsch. "Mr. Brown will be keeping you company throughout the rest of the night. From time to time, he'll find it necessary to ask you questions concerning the operation of this apartment building. You'll answer them concisely and truthfully, or you'll die. Do I make myself clear?"

"Yeah."

The desk phone rang, filling the room with its strident clamor. After the third ring, Dreyse picked up the phone and said, "Lake Point Tower Apartments." He listened to the man's voice at the other end for a moment. "Yes, sir," he said smoothly. "I'll have someone right on it." He put the receiver down and looked up. "Ortmann."

"Yes, sir."

Dreyse's smile was thin, tinged with real humor. "There's a man in 2103 who's having some difficulties with his cable reception. See to it."

"Yes, sir." Confusion registered on Ortmann's face. "But there's a storm out there, sir. There may not be much I can do about it."

"If you can't and the gentleman isn't willing to listen to reason, do something about the gentleman."

Ortmann nodded and moved out.

Dreyse looked back at the clerk and Pfirsch. "For the moment, this apartment building will offer a higher grade of services than the residents normally receive. At least, until it no longer suits our purposes. Pfirsch, you know where I'll be if you need me."

The man nodded.

"If the clerk gives you too much trouble or refuses to comply with you, kill him."

The big man swallowed hard.

Dreyse led the way out of the office, feeling lighter. The parameters of the operation had been secured around the city, and the only trouble had been with Moltke's last abduction. With the storm, with the violence that existed within Chicago on a daily basis, he felt secure that law-enforcement people wouldn't tumble to their presence much earlier than what would be necessary.

In the elevator, Vogelsang used the special key from the doorman's ring that allowed the cage to rise to the top floor without stopping along the way. As it shot up smoothly, the men in Dreyse's group unleathered silenced pistols and held them at the ready.

Dreyse shrugged his way out of the overcoat, transferring the SIG-Sauers to the double shoulder-holster rig he wore, then draped it over his arm. He brushed a few wrinkles from his dark pin-striped Brooks Brothers suit and surveyed himself in the reflection of the elevator control panel—tall and broad, handsome, with short, wiry red hair and a curly red beard. He could have been an artist, judging from the depth of his eyes or the slender length of his hands. His carriage and the way he wore the suit spoke of a quiet ability to move within business circles.

He grinned at the contradictory thoughts, all of which had been expressed to him by women he'd known over the years. None of them had ever guessed his true profession, never guessed that in his hands death was both an art and a business.

The elevator chimed just before the twin doors opened, and the men positioned in front of the cage stepped out, leveling their weapons. Dreyse heard the silenced coughs of 9 mm pistols as his hand touched the knot of his tie. The two uniformed policeman in the hallway went down with bullets through their hearts before either had a chance to draw his weapon. The elevator emptied as the rest of the group moved to secure the floor.

Dreyse walked past the first two doors because the apartments were empty. His quarry was in the back, in a unit overlooking Lake Michigan.

A policeman carrying a tray with three foam cups walked around the corner. The man's eyes widened in surprise a heartbeat before a burst from Vogelsang's Uzi knocked him to the floor.

"They've set up a coffee station," Dreyse observed as he looked down at the corpse amid the scattered and leaking cups. "That's something new." He motioned Vogelsang forward as he drew one of the SIG-Sauers and waved the rest of the team to the wall.

A moment later Vogelsang's voice rang out. "Secure."

Dreyse turned the corner and found the door he searched for. He stood beside it patiently as Vogelsang worked on the lock. It clicked back hollowly.

"Hey, Joey," a man's voice called, "is that you?"

No light showed under the edge of the door.

Dreyse knew the light from the hallway would give them away the instant they pushed the door open. He rapped on the door and said, "Coffee."

"Sounds great," the man replied.

Dreyse placed his thumb over the peephole and waited.

"Hey, Joey, what the hell's going on out there?"

Without hesitation, Dreyse fired four rounds through the door at the five-foot line. He stepped back, letting Vogelsang have the point position.

The door moved inward, then stopped, held by a security chain. Drawing his foot back, Vogelsang kicked at a spot even with the chain. The bolts wrenched free of the woodwork, then the terrorist was inside, Uzi held at waist level.

"Clear," Vogelsang called.

Dreyse entered the room and put his weapon away, knowing his targets this time would be unarmed.

The bedroom was wreathed in quiet snores and the lung-biting taste of powdered perfume. He stood in the doorway, letting his eyes adjust to the darkness.

The two figures on the bed slept apart under the blankets, the way old married couples sometimes did. Lamps sat on either side of the bed. He moved without making a sound, coming to a stop first on the woman's side and looking down at her. She was twenty or thirty pounds overweight, with curly gray hair and sagging breasts that threatened to spill out of her nightgown. He paused to pull the blanket up over the woman, not wanting to divide her attention between embarrassment and fear.

The man looked like he was in his sixties, but Dreyse knew he was actually only fifty-two and had just had a birthday two months, three weeks and two days ago. He was thin, shallow-chested, with a waxy complexion. The top of his head was bald, white fringe clinging to the sides, matching the mustache below.

Dreyse walked to the window, donned a mask and drew the curtain back, letting in the reflected light from the whirling snow.

The man snorted, jerked to wakefulness and grabbed for the glasses on his nightstand as he switched on the light. Shock covered his features as Dreyse turned into the light so the man could see him. "Who the hell are you and what are you doing here?" the man demanded, taking care to keep the blanket over his wife.

The woman started, then turned over in bed to blink owlishly at Dreyse. She said something under her breath as she tried to take cover under the blanket.

"Who I am shall have to remain my secret. As to what I'm doing here, I came to announce the terms of the ransom for your city, Mr. Mayor, and to prove to you that you should see to it your constituents are exceedingly generous." He smiled. "Believe me, they'll have plenty of other reasons to be."

2

"So far," Brognola said, "there have been no clues about the identity of these guys. They're quiet, they're quick and they don't give a damn how many people get hurt."

Bolan continued leafing through the photographs the Justice man had brought, mixing pictures with memory. Then he put the photos away, turning his gaze on the black night hanging over Dulles airport. "What about their dead?"

"If there have been any, they've taken the bodies with them."

"Nobody knows if one of these people have been put down?"

"No one alive."

"The hostages couldn't provide descriptions?"

"No. Their captors wore masks, then the hostages' eyes were taped shut and they were kept captive in their own homes. The ones who lived."

"How did they get into the cities?"

"We're not sure. Crime teams in Dallas and San Francisco are still working on that."

"The least noticeable method would be to drive in."

"Yeah, we thought of that, but that would mean—"

"That they have a base of operations inside the United States."

Brognola nodded. "A lot of people aren't happy with that line of thinking."

"Has Aaron checked the car-rental agencies around those cities? It's possible these people flew into different airports and rented cars."

"We've gone round and round with that one, and invested a lot of man-hours checking it out. We got zilch. Assuming they did rent cars, any left behind would stick out. Aaron accessed hundreds of stolen-car reports without discovering a goddamned thing."

"Whoever arranged this might have set up some kind of bulk pickup operation."

"It's a possibility. The problem is that right now there are a lot of possibilities, and they all make some kind of sense."

"And every move they make has been well researched. They may be moving on a city a month, but you can bet they've worked on the plans a hell of a lot longer than that."

"There's no doubt about it. These guys are staking out some of the wealthier and more influential people in their target cities, taking their time to make sure everything runs by the numbers when they kick the operation into play. They know who to pick, and they know when to pick them." Brognola tapped the stack of photographs. "They like to pick the big people, people who have an influence on municipal governments, people who work in the state legislatures."

"How long does the occupation last?" Bolan noticed his friend's wince at the military term, then realized his own mind was turning more and more in that direction, too. It was why he'd requested the heavy ordnance, and it was why Brognola had voiced no objections about filling the order.

"Estimates are from twelve to sixteen hours. They're in and out of these damned cities like clockwork."

"That's pretty much the way I've got it figured. Money is the only motivation?"

"It's the only thing that figures. The media people have gotten a whiff of what's going on behind the scenes, but the people directly involved aren't talking. Some of the other family members are repeating some of what happened, but nothing is coming from the folks who lost family to these bastards. The President gave them his word that we'd get rid of these terrorists before they struck again."

"How much money are we talking about?"

"Millions."

Bolan studied the faces of the pictures again, seeing the blood, seeing the tears in the eyes of the people around the dead, feeling their pain, stoking the anger that burned inside him. "This isn't going to be an easy one to soft-sell, Hal."

"I know. The Man figures this is a high-priority, high-risk situation, explosive no matter how you handle it, and even more destructive if we don't take some kind of stand against these bastards. People are dying, and we haven't been able to do a goddamned thing about it the way the PDs and special units are set up. This is a military operation, terrorism on American soil. Wonderland is worried if the media does break this story, we're going to have a national panic on our hands."

"There's only one way to end this." Bolan stared into his friend's eyes, looking for some sort of hesitation that might be there from Washington and the powers that be.

Brognola returned his gaze full-measure. "I know. These guys have to be made an example. There's no way we can keep it from the press after the shit hits the fan in Chicago, but we want to offer a statement of our own that's written in the body-count language these guys deal in."

So they'd turned to the best body-count specialist they knew. Bolan let the thought pass through him, noting the pain in Brognola's eyes, knowing his friend was aware he had stripped war down to its essentials in front of a man who'd been forced by his own personal convictions to take the trade on as his life's work.

Brognola looked away. "You can step away from this, you know."

"I know, but you know I won't."

"We don't even know how many men are involved in this, Striker. You could be signing your own death warrant by simply setting foot in Chicago."

"There'll be other names ahead of mine," Bolan said lightly. "The list could be even longer if I don't take a hand."

"That's the only reason I agreed to be liaison on something I consider to be a suicide mission. That, and I knew you'd involve yourself anyway." He took a manila envelope from the stack of files. "Your ID's in here. You're getting a cover identity from Aaron and me, a bullet-proofing of that identity by the State Department and military people, and a blank check from the President for everything you need and everything you do. The Man wants these guys taken down, Striker, and taken down hard.''

Bolan unsealed the envelope and poured the ID out. He looked at the Virginia driver's license with his picture on it. Under it was the name Thomas Fox with an address in Fairfax. He took his wallet from one of his personal duffels and put the license in the appropriate empty slot, adding the FBI ID that identified him as a special agent assigned to VICAP, the Violent Criminal Apprehension Program that pursued serial killers. Except for the times his operations were sanctioned through the government, the only thing the wallet carried was money. ''VICAP?'' he asked as he looked back at Brognola.

''Best we could come up with that wouldn't raise too many questions. The Fox identity states that you're a specialist in military matters. There's already a VICAP team in Chicago, flown in less than an hour ago. They've been advised of your arrival, but have been told that you'll be operating independently, though with substantial authority. We haven't been able to assemble a team for you. Phoenix Force is overseas, and Able Team is tied up in L.A.''

''This isn't a team show,'' Bolan said as he flipped open the cover on Thomas Fox's personal records.

''You're also going to be penetrating the Chicago PD's defenses, because they're not going to willingly allow a wild card in their midst while the hostage situation is in full swing. If you can't keep a low profile, you're going to become a target for them, too, and the Man won't be able to step in to cover your ass once you're blown.''

"I have the feeling when that happens we're all going to have too much to do with the team behind this to worry about me," the warrior stated grimly. He put the Fox record aside and dug in his duffel bag, coming away with the small but thick Ops journal he'd put together on the Dallas and San Francisco strikes, adding only a little from Brognola's intel to the small store of concrete knowledge he'd accumulated through personal observation. The whole thing felt military: the timing, the execution, the killings and the fade-in, fade-out routine. It wouldn't have surprised him to learn the leader of the unknown group had a personal journal along the lines of his on the heart and soul of Chicago. He glanced back up from the pages and asked Brognola for a list of the city's possible hostage targets.

"DOESN'T LOOK like a city under siege, does it?" Brognola asked, peering over Bolan's shoulder as the Lear circled into the sparse air traffic filtering through Meigs Field.

A blanket of white snow covered Chicago, turning the tall buildings into cruel fingers thrusting at the dark sky. Lake Michigan was a forbidding, black surface broken only by the docks and boats along Lake Shore Drive. Traffic was light, sparse caravans of yellow headlights and ruby taillights, and moved slowly.

"By the weather, maybe," Bolan said, removing the multiple-band headset that connected him with the pilot, radio and television stations, and law-enforcement channels. He placed his hand on the glass, felt the chill that soaked through. He looked at the big Fed. "The cop wounded at the lake kidnapping died on the table a half hour ago."

Brognola sat back in his seat. "Damn."

"That brings the total to five down."

"What about the Ellison girl?"

"Vanessa Ellison is still listed as missing, but no demands have been made of her father. At least none that he's talking about."

"How's the media carrying it?"

"As a one-shot kidnapping so far, but a few reporters have indicated that the story may be deeper than they can release now. Police liaisons are handing out a lot of 'no comments.'"

Brognola shook his head. "A media blackout isn't going to solve their problem. That's like an ostrich sticking its head in the sand. Your ass is still wide open to get the hell kicked out of it."

"This team knows what it's doing. Once the truth of this hits the news, can you imagine what things are going to be like for the rest of the people? Most of them are going to be sitting in the night wondering if an unanswered phone means one of their family has been taken or killed. The families that know they're directly involved are going to be putting pressure on to keep the situation from going ballistic, and you can bet the team has chosen its targets with care. Vanessa Ellison is the daughter of Carter Ellison."

"The motel king?"

Bolan tapped the files on the floor between his feet. "Yeah, but Ellison's also on the city police board and has donated generously to Chicago's Fraternal Order of Police. There are people who are going to be plenty willing to listen to what Ellison has to say, and he's not going to want them to rush in where angels fear to tread."

"Yeah." Brognola popped an antacid tablet.

"I'M GOING WITH YOU as far as the police command post," Brognola said, swinging the last of Bolan's special equipment cases into the cargo area of the full-size Chevy Blazer 4WD that had been waiting at Meigs Field in Special Agent Fox's name. "I'll give you an introduction, make sure you're logged as a friendly, then slip you back into the field."

Clouds of fog belched from the tail pipe of the Blazer, swept away by the freezing winds. Piles of snow left over from the yellow minidozers working the airport crunched under Bolan's boots.

Clad in jeans, a blue-and-black-checked flannel shirt, a black watch cap and a sheepskin jacket and gloves, Bolan knew he could blend in to the background of the city as needed. The blacksuit was an added layer of insulation under the street clothes. He kept the Beretta snugged in shoulder leather, and rigged a holster under the Blazer's dashboard on the steering console for the Desert Eagle, hanging it where he could reach it quickly but where it wouldn't be readily visible.

"You may find yourself in a tough position if this thing turns sour," Bolan warned.

Brognola gave him a quick grin. "Hell, tough positions were created with me in mind. That's why I get paid all those big bucks."

Bolan chuckled then resumed visual inspection of his latest piece of equipment ordered through the Justice Department for his current operation. With the weather conditions being what they were in Chicago, and given the nature of the men he stalked, he'd known special transport was called for.

The Blazer was full-size, riding tall on snow tires, an imposing tank that would see him through the worst the storm had to offer. He'd drawn the line at having chains put on the wheels, because a link could break at a crucial moment and beat hell out of the body, letting people know for miles that he was coming. He'd settled for the spiked tires and the powerful winch mounted in front to keep him mobile. Heavy iron bars had been welded on to the front and back, close enough together to keep bullets from puncturing the radiator or from coming through the back and hitting the jerricans of gasoline stocked there.

A police radio and CB were mounted overhead, and a mobile phone was connected to the dash between the seats. The glove compartment held a battery-operated cherry with a magnetic base if he needed official recognition on the street. The engine under the hood was a powerful V-8, and the whole vehicle sat on a specially tuned suspension that would give him the best performance possible on the snow and ice. It had taken some string-pulling from Brognola's end, but the garage had delivered it less than half an hour ago.

The Executioner clambered up into the driver's seat as Brognola hoisted himself aboard. Switching on the wipers, he dusted the melting snow from the windshield and put the stick in first, finding the friction point of the clutch as a minidozer rattled by in front of him. He looked over his shoulder and saw the Lear sitting cold where Travis had taxied it.

"Wayne's a good man," Brognola said as he poured coffee from a thermos into a foam cup.

"That's the impression I got," Bolan replied as he let out the clutch. The big tires grabbed the uneven terrain and the Blazer bobbed toward the exit gates. He took the half cup of coffee Brognola held out.

"He's going to be at your disposal until this operation is completed."

"Thanks." He reached overhead and switched the radio on to an all-news station.

Brognola grimaced.

"Where's the meet?" Bolan steered through the gates and pulled onto the street. He opened the glove compartment, produced a street map of inner Chicago, folded it, then used small magnets to fasten it to the glove compartment lid. The compartment light illuminated the streets when he switched it on. He'd studied the street names during the flight from Dulles, along with the other information the big Fed had brought. He shifted into third as he built up speed, feeling the tires buck across the ruts left by earlier traffic.

"The Chicago PD." Brognola didn't sound happy about it.

Checking the traffic ahead and behind him, Bolan shifted down and used the Blazer's four-wheel drive to crunch up over the median of piled snow and ice left by the city's clearing efforts and pass the sedan before him. He cut back in front of the car at a safe distance, noticing the way the vehicle behind him edged up on the sedan. He sipped his coffee, keeping a flickering visual scan on the two pairs of headlights behind him. "Who's ramrodding the local show?"

"A guy named Roland Quartermain. He's on the mayor's Crime Task Force Review Board and has a lot of stroke with the precincts."

"He's a civilian?"

Brognola nodded. "From what I hear, he's done an admirable job attempting to clean up the drug problem in the inner city."

"This is more sophisticated than that."

"I know, but the guy seems to really care about what he does."

"Civilians who care can sometimes get you killed even faster than noncivilians who don't," the Executioner said grimly. He stepped harder on the accelerator, and distance started to build between him and the sedan, pinning the trailing vehicle behind it.

"The good thing about Quartermain is that he does have that support," Brognola replied. "Otherwise we'd be facing an undisciplined disaster here."

"It may get to that, anyway." Bolan took the first right he came to, downshifting as he plunged the Blazer forward.

"State Street isn't this way," Brognola protested.

Finishing his coffee, the Executioner dropped the cup behind the seat and said, "Belt up, guy. We've got company."

The big Fed reached for the seat belt without looking over his shoulder.

Bolan steered with both hands, watching as their pursuer made the corner. It was some kind of van, he could make that out now, but the interior was dark and let him know the driver had intentionally switched off the console lights.

Consulting his map, Bolan made a left and shifted back down as he headed for Michigan Avenue. Facts and figures from his readings and map study trickled through his thoughts. The Chicago Police Department was south on State Street not far from their position, but he wanted to pull the action as far away from the local law-enforcement people as possible. Michigan Avenue had received much of the attention given by the snow crews and was relatively clear.

He turned north, marking his course for the Michigan Avenue Bridge. His rearview mirror caught the bouncing lights of the van as it swung around the corner and pursued. Reaching overhead, he turned down the radio volume.

"They're not giving up," Brognola said from the passenger seat. He held a snub-nosed .38 in his lap.

Bolan didn't reply, keeping his mind and reflexes cued for the two-tiered bridge coming up. The structure rose up out of the darkness with a suddenness he wasn't expecting. He kept his foot on the accelerator, trusting the four-wheel drive. The Blazer bounced as it gained the bridge, and the steel beams shot by, glazed for split seconds by the headlights. The Chicago River was a black ribbon stretching east and west under the bridge.

Oncoming traffic pulled as far to the right as possible as he sped toward it. The van's headlights filled the rearview mirror. A white-yellow-orange bouquet bloomed beside the van as the dulled thunder of autofire penetrated the Blazer's interior. Ricochets sparked from the rear bumper guard.

"Hold tight," Bolan warned as he tracked from side to side as much as he dared under the existing weather conditions. "We're about to show them this rabbit has fangs."

Brognola braced against the dash.

The Blazer roared off the bridge yards ahead of the van. Bolan cut the wheels sharply as he disengaged the four-wheel drive. Controlling the resulting skid, he downshifted to second, let the rear end float around and reengaged the four-wheel drive on the fly, bringing the Blazer around in a 180-degree turn. The maneuver was sloppy on the snow, but serviceable.

"Ready?" Bolan asked as he gunned the engine and slid the stick into first.

"As I'm going to be."

The driver of the van realized too late what his quarry had done, throwing the vehicle off balance in the snow when he tried to brake.

Bolan let off on the clutch and engaged the gears, gathering speed as he picked his spot. The front of the Blazer slammed into the rear of the Volkswagen van just behind center, rocking it off the two left-side wheels and bringing it to a sudden stop. Double-clutching, the Executioner fed fuel to the powerful V-8 engine, shoving the van in a shrill embrace toward the metal guardrails on that side of the street.

The van hit hard. Reversing, Bolan steered his vehicle away, switching off the engine and leaving the keys in the ignition.

Moving by instinct now, his eyes still on the van, he unlatched the case containing the SPAS-15 and brought it out as figures erupted from the van.

Cold air cut into the Executioner's face as he shoved his door open, aware that Brognola had already taken the offensive. Ice crunched underfoot as he ran.

Headlight beams illuminated the area in patchwork fashion, yellow lines of demarcation overlaying the black and white of the night. Bolan flicked off the safety and brought the SPAS-15 up to his shoulder as two men came around the front of the van.

Hollow pops from Brognola's .38 punctuated the rattling autofire that came from the van.

Bolan caught a glimpse of the big Fed in a Weaver T-stance, leveling the snub-nosed revolver for another shot. The Executioner's finger tightened on the SPAS's trigger as he centered the weapon on the chest of the first gunner. Muzzle-flash jetted from the barrel of the semiautomatic shotgun and the man was blown backward. The warrior targeted the second man less than a heartbeat later, stroking the trigger and directing his fire at the guy's head. The man tumbled to the ground, unmistakably dead.

Autofire raked through the snow, scattering clumps of ice to glitter like miniature rainbows in the glare of headlights coming both ways down Michigan Avenue.

"They're wearing Kevlar bodysuits," Bolan shouted to Brognola as he took shelter behind the Blazer.

Hunkered behind the fender on the other side, the big Fed nodded, finishing up with a speed-loader and snapping the cylinder into place. "Masks and helmets are made of Kevlar, too."

The van's engine chugged to stubborn life, and the headlights shivered as it idled. Metal screamed as it struggled to rip free of the railings.

Bolan emptied the clip across the van's windshield and into the tires visible to him. Bullets ricocheted off the bumper of the Blazer and shattered headlights and windows. The warrior reloaded the SPAS with his only spare clip.

Shattered hunks of glass erupted through the crumpled windshield of the van, propelled by the driver's assault rifle.

The front of the Blazer sagged as a handful of rounds punctured the tire on Brognola's side.

More shadows joined the first outside the van, taking up positions.

The Executioner's next round from the SPAS-15 caught another of their attackers full in the mask as the man peered around the front of the van. The double-aught buckshot yanked the man into the open, skidding him on his back across the snow. "Hal."

Turning at the sound of his name, Brognola caught the butt of the military shotgun as Bolan slid it across the hood.

The Executioner reached back inside the Blazer, aware that only seconds remained before the men tried to overrun their position. He unlocked an equipment case and took out two grenades. Whirling back to his position, he pulled the pins, counted down a second, then hurled them at the tires of the immobilized van. He yelled a warning to Brognola and drew the Beretta.

Two of the five men huddled by the vehicle evidently recognized the movement for what it was and tried to escape. The double tap of the twin explosions blew them from their feet, arcing the resultant flames of the van's ruptured gas tank after them. Fire caught in their clothing and blazed brightly.

The van buckled from the explosions. The doors hung on their hinges as the flames shot skyward. Another eruption, this one stronger than the previous two, gutted the Volkswagen and let Bolan know there'd been firepower aboard that their attackers hadn't been able to bring into play. Flames crackled and spit from the wreckage of the vehicle and from the bodies sprawled around it. Nothing moved.

Taking time to retrieve the Desert Eagle from the steering column, Bolan moved forward with Brognola covering his flank. The closest body was fifteen feet from the burning van. Knowing there might be more explosive materials aboard the vehicle, he rolled the body over with a foot to extinguish the fire clinging to its back. Snow sizzled. Using his teeth and keeping the big .44 ready at his hip, he pulled on a glove from his pocket, then hooked his fingers in the burned jacket the corpse wore and pulled.

The dead man slid easily across the snow-covered street.

Brognola came forward at his approach, the SPAS-15 pointed at the sky. He looked down at the corpse as Bolan used his Ka-bar to cut the charred mask from the face. The Kevlar fell to one side, revealing more charring underneath. The sweet smell of burned flesh shot through with toasted vinyl filled the air. The big Fed took a handkerchief from a pocket and held it over his nose and mouth. "We're not going to be able to ID this guy."

Bolan shook his head and turned back to look at the van. Flames soared a dozen feet above it, the night sky glittering with brightly burning embers that winked into and out of life. "No, and you can bet this is as good as it gets."

The Executioner lowered the Desert Eagle, looking over the battle zone. "These guys are prepared for war, Hal, and they've cut in to your security."

"I know." Brognola's voice was gruff. "I read this as a message, but why us?"

Bolan looked at his friend, sure of the answer because his combat senses verified it. "Justice represents the unknown in their operation. It means they've either got somebody on the inside in this city, or they think they have enough intel on the local heroes to neuter them before they can attempt to fight back. The FBI's VICAP team came in alone, without me. You've got a prominent position in Wonderland and undoubtedly represent a vested interest in what goes down here. My late inclusion in the operation made me stand out, too." He looked at the smoldering bodies as sirens knifed through the air. "This was strictly a take-out-and-terrorize hit that would move a lot of messages through the channels."

Patrol cars swung into view at both ends of the bridge, cherries flashing.

Brognola laid the SPAS-15 on top of the tilted Blazer.

The patrol cars skidded to unsure stops, and uniformed officers kicked their doors open, leveling their weapons at Bolan and Brognola.

The warrior held his hands well away from his body, the Desert Eagle dangling from a forefinger. A sour grin twisted Brognola's lips as he glanced at his friend. "This isn't quite the introduction to the Chicago Police Department I had in mind."

3

"Up against the car," a rough male voice commanded. "Keep your hands where we can see them." The fire raging through the metal skeleton of the van blazed up, throwing an orange cast over the assembled ranks of Chicago's Finest.

Mack Bolan moved slowly, complying with the orders. He placed the Desert Eagle on top of the Blazer's roof, then stepped away from it and put his hands on the hood. Brognola stood on the other side, hands spread out as well.

Footsteps crunched across the snow, louder than the cracklings and poppings still coming from the van. "You just move easy there, big fella," a man's voice said softly into his ear. "My buddy's name is Al. You can't see him from where you are, but I promise you— any sudden moves and Al will take the top of your head off, no questions asked. You understand?"

"Yes," Bolan replied. His peripheral vision showed the black cop returning his handgun to his holster and buttoning it in tight. Another set of uniformed policemen were handcuffing Brognola.

"Okay, big fella, you stick your left hand back here. Real slow, you understand?"

Bolan did as he was instructed. Metal bit into his wrist, and he heard the familiar racheting sounds of handcuffs.

"Now the right one."

Once the handcuffs were in place, the cop bent Bolan over the hood of the Blazer. He studied the orange tongues of flame reflected in the spiderwebbed glass of the 4WD. Impatience chapped at him worse than the wind. Even though the assault had failed to produce the desired results, the ensuing police investigation would delay him taking the battle back to the people responsible, immersing him in the agonizingly slow legal system.

"Got a shoulder rig here, Al," the first cop said, relieving the Executioner of the Beretta. He handed it back as he had the Desert Eagle. The frisk continued, and Bolan had to give the guy credit for his thoroughness. Magazines for the Beretta and big Israeli-made .44 turned up in other hidden pockets in the sheepskin coat, as well as the reserve in the shoulder rig. The uniformed policeman slipped two metal rings with piano wire tied between them out of another pocket.

"Garrote," the unseen man said. "You play rough, don't you, fella?"

Bolan didn't say anything. Brognola's frisk had come up negative except for a couple of speed-loaders for the .38. The big Fed was being hustled toward a patrol car.

The cop doing the frisk dropped to one knee to continue down each of Bolan's legs. "You really come loaded for bear when you come to town, don't you?"

Bolan ignored the jibe, feeling the bounce of the Blazer's hood under him as two more policemen clambered through the rear deck of the vehicle.

The frisk revealed the Ka-bar sheathed in one of the cowboy boots Bolan wore.

"Keith?"

"Yeah, Al?" the uniformed officer asked as he got to his feet.

"A guy this cute, I think I'd check his belt. You notice he dresses the cowboy part, but he isn't wearing one of those shitkicker belts with his name on it."

The officer released Bolan's belt and removed the buckle. A smile spread across his face when the belt knife gleamed in the firelight. He held it out. "Where'd you get this? The back pages of one of those Saturday-night street-survivalist magazines?"

Bolan disregarded the questions, trying to put himself in the mind of a man who'd sent the wrecking crew out. Would he have someone watching, or would he have backed a play that wasn't supposed to have been busted?

"Strong, silent type, aren't you?" the cop said, reaching into Bolan's back pocket for his wallet.

"Hey," one of the policemen in the Blazer called. "There's cases of heavy assault weapons in here, and all of them marked with Department of Justice ID."

The cop straightened Bolan to a standing position by tugging on the handcuffs, then turned him around and stared at him. "You a Fed?"

"ID's in the wallet. Why don't you take a look for yourself."

The cop's grin showed no humor.

A tall black man dressed in a dark woolen cap, gray sweatshirt, jeans, a long leather coat and expensive boots came toward Bolan and the two police officers. "I'll take that," the man said, holding out a hand for the wallet.

The policeman dropped the wallet into the other man's hand grudgingly.

The man flipped open the wallet, which looked small in his big hands. A gust of cold wind shuffled the open coat to one side, revealing a Smith & Wesson stainless steel .357 Combat Magnum with a four-inch barrel in a cross-draw hip holster. A detective's shield gleamed briefly to the right of center on the belt supporting the .357.

Bolan studied the man's dark features, realizing the poor light given off by the Volkswagen bonfire gave the guy years he hadn't marked yet. The detective still had a couple to go before he tagged thirty.

"You read Mr. Fox his rights?" the detective asked, looking up from the wallet. He closed it and put it inside a coat pocket.

"Not yet, Detective Trebeck," the uniformed cop said with rancor in his voice. "But we were about to take care of that very thing."

"I'll take care of it for you."

"Now wait just a goddamned minute," the uniformed cop protested. He pointed to Bolan. "This is our collar. You're not going to waltz in here and take this guy away from us."

Trebeck's face was impassive. "If you're looking for an excuse to get back to the station to warm your ass, Officer Cliburn, let me clue you in on something—this isn't going to be it. Did you even check this guy's ID?"

"I was about to do that when you walked up."

Trebeck lowered his voice. "Then let me introduce you. Officer Cliburn, meet Special Agent Fox of the FBI. Maybe that explains the Department of Justice tags you guys found on the equipment cases in the Blazer."

The patrolmen looked at Bolan. The one holding the gun put it away; the other spit on the ground. "A fuckin' Feeb? He doesn't dress like any Feeb I ever saw."

Trebeck put his hands in his pockets. "Maybe you haven't seen them all."

The man scowled.

"Now, why don't you get the hell out of the way before you do anything else to hamper working conditions between the city of Chicago and the Department of Justice. You can go toast your ass over there by that burning van. Just make sure you don't go stumbling around over the evidence the on-site teams will be trying to recover."

"Fuck you, Trebeck." The cop stalked off.

Trebeck smiled. "That's fuck you, *Sergeant* Trebeck. I want a report of this incident to hit my desk within two hours."

The cop waved it away.

"Now, Agent Fox," the detective said, "why don't we get in out of the cold and get to know each other better."

Bolan noticed there was no offer to remove the handcuffs. He followed Trebeck to an unmarked dark blue sedan. "Where's Brognola?"

"Your partner?" Trebeck asked as he held the rear door of the sedan open. He was at least two inches taller than Bolan's own six-three.

The Executioner sat in the rear seat with difficulty.

"Your partner's with my partner." Trebeck shut the door and got in the front seat. He switched on the ignition and turned the heater on high.

"Your partner has his own car, too?" Bolan asked.

Trebeck shook his head and grinned. "Hell, no. The Chicago Police Department isn't funded as well as the people you work for. We don't come equipped with rocket launchers and shit."

A yellow fire engine, the sirens whining, drove through the parked ranks of patrol cars. Even before it came to a full stop, men wearing yellow slickers dropped off and started pulling at hoses. The harsh static of the police radio provided background noise as Bolan and Trebeck watched the hoses spray to life.

"I got a problem with you, Fox," Trebeck said, shifting his attention back to Bolan. "Something about you don't ring quite true."

Bolan remained silent, his mind more on the developing situation in the city than the one in the car.

"ID is cheap to come by," Trebeck went on. "For the right kind of cash I can be anybody I want to be."

"If you have a problem with the ID, call it in."

"Not that simple, my man." Depths shifted in the dark eyes, revealing glints of the intellect hidden behind the easy manner and street accent. "I already had you checked out. You and your partner came back clean as a whistle, even decked out in some kind of high-level security clearance to get involved here. You maxed out on well-wishers, homeboy, but it got me asking myself why.'' He smoothed his pencil-thin mustache.

"Me and Jack took a peek at the dossier on you and Brognola when it came in a few hours ago. Found out they rated you high as a fix-it man in the Feebs.'' The humor had disappeared from Trebeck's face. ''Gave me a real uncomfortable itch when I found out you were a GI Joe expert.''

One of the firemen stumbled away from a charred body and threw up.

''Must be a new guy,'' Trebeck commented. He waved toward the body. ''That kind of shit bother you, Agent Fox?''

Bolan shook his head. He glanced at the parked cars behind the unmarked unit, trying to find Brognola, wondering if the big Fed was being submerged in the same territorial battle between law-enforcement divisions as he was.

''Didn't think so. I noticed that a body got itself dragged over toward your Blazer.'' He looked back at Bolan. ''You know the guy?''

''No.''

Trebeck smiled. ''Wouldn't tell me if you did, would you?''

''Depends.''

''Yeah. At least you're honest about it. Most of the Feeb force would look you square in the eye, straighten their Brooks Brothers suits and lie their tight little asses off. See, that's why me and Jack decided to involve ourselves in this tonight, kind of put together a little fact-finding mission while we made sure nobody blew your heads off so soon after you hit town.''

''Your bit for community service?''

Trebeck laughed. "You could call it that, and you could call it good PR work." He shifted in the seat, turning the police band down. "The thing is, Agent Fox, me and Jack grew up in this city. We got lives and family here, a few hundred girls that haven't been blessed by our charms yet. We belong here. We're not outsiders like you and the rest of the Federal Task Force that's busy waving their balls around while they try to take control of what's going down here tonight."

"We're after the same thing."

A scowl darkened Trebeck's face. "The hell we are. You guys come down here with your John Wayne hats on, looking to even the score for what happened in San Francisco and Dallas." He pointed at the exploded van. "You guys figure to do whatever you can to stop these clowns this time. I know. I've heard some of the talk in the ranks myself. The way I see it, you guys would resurrect Old Lady O'Leary's cow to get the job done if that's what it took tonight, and leave us here in the ashes."

"How do you propose to handle it?"

"We aren't going to back off, homeboy, if that's what you're thinking. This is our turf. If those bastards can be taken down, you can bet your sweet ass that we'll be the guys who can get it done. You can tell that to all your buddies when you see them." Trebeck paused. "And you can tell them for me that if they cross the line, any of them, a lot of the guys in the PD like me aren't about to turn our heads and look the other way. Understand?"

"Yeah."

"Good, now get out of the car. I've got work to do."

Trebeck opened the door and Bolan stepped back into the winter air. The cutting chill seemed a few degrees warmer than the cold shoulder the detective gave him as he folded back under the steering wheel. He watched the detective pull away, tapping the brakes gently as he stopped to pick up another man.

A uniformed man answered Trebeck's call, leaned into the open window for a moment, then walked toward Bolan with a scowl on his face. "Sergeant Trebeck says you people gotta move your vehicle because you're blocking official police business." The patrolman unlocked the handcuffs and removed them. "I'll have your gear released and returned."

Bolan was pulling the spare tire from the rear deck of the Blazer when Brognola joined him.

"You get the same kind of speech I did?" the big Fed asked.

The tire bounced as it hit the ground, trying to shoot off to one side. Bolan controlled it easily and rolled it to the front of the Blazer. "If you mean the get-out-of-town-before-sundown one, then yeah, I got it."

"That's the one." Brognola unwrapped a cigar and stuck it into his mouth. Angry fires danced in his eyes. "If we're not careful on this one, we're going to be working out of the center of a cross fire."

"Bet on it," Bolan said as he returned with the jack and lug wrench. He dropped to one knee to loosen the nuts holding the tire, feeling the cold wetness of the snow-covered street soak into his pants. He twisted the first nut loose, moved on to the next. "Whoever planned this figured on these results. After San Francisco and Dallas, he knew federal reaction time would be a lot quicker. Justice had geared up for him and was ready to field an army. The only way he could out-maneuver the machine was to make sure the effort was fragmented.''

"Politics." Brognola's scowl deepened.

"Maybe later," Bolan replied as he jacked up the front end of the Blazer. "Right now he's just using territorial aggression against us and the home team. This city is going to be filled with hostile guns, theirs, those of the people of Chicago and Justice's. There's going to be a very fine line between right and wrong, and it's going to get thinner with every dead hostage that turns up."

"If we had more time," Brognola said, "we could work out a better situation, figure out a system to pool our resources."

Bolan dropped the bullet-shredded tire and slipped the spare into place, then put the nuts back on. "The problem is, this guy isn't going to give anybody time. Whenever he thinks there's a lull in the action, he'll put more pressure on, drop another body into the street."

Bolan spoke quietly as he tapped the wheel cover back into place, convinced of his words. "No matter which way this one is played out, it's going to be a lot worse than San Francisco or Dallas."

ONCE THE PRELIMINARY introductions were done at the police department headquarters, Bolan took a back seat to the action, watching as federal and local law-enforcement divisions tried to coordinate their activities. Information was still coming in over the fax machines concerning the Volkswagen van the Executioner had put down at the bridge less than an hour ago, but none of it contained any worthwhile data. The plates had belonged to a 1977 Monte Carlo listed with the Department of Motor Vehicles in Chicago, and the owner hadn't known when they'd been taken. The vehicle serial numbers on the dashboard and the engine hadn't been traced. No identification had been possible on the fire-ravaged bodies recovered at the scene.

Circulating through the crowded room, Bolan scanned the information posted along the walls. The lists of suspected hostages seemed to grow every few minutes. The phones never stopped ringing. Cigarette smoke filled the air, giving a hazy appearance to the fluorescent light tubes overhead. He smelled the sour stench of fear that had gathered in the rooms and felt the oppressive uselessness of waiting.

Chicago was starting to come alive with the fear, too. The media had already splashed pictures of the burned-out van across television sets, made even more ominous by the obvious hedging by police department spokesmen answering questions. A couple of the film crews had even made it to the scene early enough to tape some of the bodies being recovered.

Pausing at a switchboard, Bolan listened to the policewoman take another call, reading the information off to the patrol car responding to it. Her fingers flew furiously as she typed it into the computer. "Charlie Niner, this is Dispatch."

"Go, Dispatch."

"The caller says he's fired two shots at the person outside his door."

"Roger, Dispatch, I have the house in sight. I see a body out front. Have your caller shove the gun through a window and stand away from the door."

"No, sir," the dispatch officer said calmly. "Those men are police officers. Throw out your weapon so they can approach the house."

"Okay, Dispatch, I see the gun. I'm moving in."

The dispatch officer was silent, fingers frozen above the keys.

"Dispatch, this is Charlie Niner. I need an ambulance. I've got a gunshot victim, unarmed, male, approximately fifteen years of age. Impact was the chest area, looks like from a 12-gauge, and there's a lot of glass from the window the charge came through."

Bolan moved away as the dispatch officer made the necessary call. The ambulance services, the fire departments' emergency teams, the hospital emergency rooms, and the police department would all be overworked tonight, and senseless death would add to the body count. Sorting through the panic calls for ones that might prove worthwhile would tax even more man-hours, and it would only increase when the terror of what was really happening gripped the city.

He came to a stop in front of the city schematic mounted on corkboard, scanning the eastern coast along Lake Michigan until he found the yellow pin signifying the area where the policemen had been killed earlier. Another pushpin, this one red, targeted Michigan Avenue where his confrontation had occurred.

He lost himself in the planning of it for a moment. Whoever the guy was who'd set the siege in motion, he had to have a network set up somewhere. There would be tie-ins to local media outlets, a base station that would monitor police and emergency bands, and a station placed high enough in the city to maintain something of an aerial surveillance. The Sears Tower came to mind immediately, followed by the John Hancock Center. Both had observation decks.

It was even possible that the siege team had been able to secure a helicopter, judging from the other hardware that had been brought in.

Considering the number of people who might or might not be hostages, Bolan decided that if he'd been calling the shots on the operation, he'd have divided them into a handful of groups. It would make them easier to control and easier to hide, and it would keep the balance of power in the right hands. He'd have also issued orders that each group wasn't to have contact with any of the others, or even know where each was located. A lot depended on how big the siege force was.

Bolan believed it was large. That would explain why so much money was needed so quickly, as well as how research was done so thoroughly in advance. With the operation set up and paying off, the terrorists could afford to keep an intelligence unit gathering information consistently.

He moved on, jostling through people in three-piece suits and people in Chicago police uniforms. Both sides, federal and local, had tagged him as an outsider. His ID and Brognola's political clout had assured him free movement through their ranks, but they saw the difference in him. He knew it was there, could feel it himself. This was a military operation and had placed him in a similar mind-set, throwing him out of step with conventional law-enforcement tactics. Where the waiting left the various departments in charley horses, the Executioner accepted it as a natural element of the operation's structure.

Out in the hall, he made his way through the fast-paced traffic and found Brognola in the little office Roland Quartermain had claimed as his own.

Brognola looked exasperated. His tie was loosened and a soggy cigar was stuck in a corner of his mouth. He acknowledged Bolan with a slight nod.

Roland Quartermain looked impeccable in a dark blue three-piece suit. He was built square and rangy, with broad, generous features that cameras were kind to, blond hair and dark hazel eyes. A lawyer by training and an athlete by preference, Quartermain paced the floor in front of his desk with one hand tucked casually in his pocket while the other punctuated his words.

"This isn't at all the kind of help we'd expected from the Justice Department," Quartermain was saying. "I was informed this expert of yours had insights into the military mind, not that he would be actively involved in the streets in war maneuvers."

"At the time," Brognola said, "there wasn't a hell of a lot of choice."

"So you've said." Quartermain shook his head, pulling a sheaf of papers from the metal desk. "Yet, your man apparently came armed for this kind of activity. Should I read you the list of weapons the police officers found in his vehicle?"

Brognola shook his head. "There's no need, Counselor. I requisitioned those items myself."

Quartermain dropped the papers on the desk, the
tight smile on his face telling Bolan that Brognola's
reference to "Counselor" had scored. "Look, Mr.
Brognola, I didn't ask you in here so we could butt our
heads together like a pair of goats. I'd hoped we could
draw some lines of understanding. The mayor en-
trusted me to take care of this city in his absence, and
I intend to do that. Without getting anyone killed."

"That's a pretty tall order, Quartermain," Bolan
said as he walked forward. "You've already lost five
policemen."

Quartermain gave him a brief stare, then perched on
the corner of his desk, hands in his pockets. "Who are
you?"

"The subject of this little discussion." Bolan returned the penetrating gaze easily, taking an instant
dislike to the man's pompousness.

"You're Fox?"

"Yes."

"Perhaps you couldn't have come at a better time,
Agent Fox. I wanted to say this to you myself, anyway, rather than have the message relayed through
Brognola and possibly diluted." Quartermain picked
the papers up from the desk and waved them at Bolan. "This report about the confrontation on Michigan Avenue Bridge concerns me gravely. According to
everything I've heard, there was a pitched gunfight
there involving military hardware."

"I don't remember being asked to file a report. Did
you, Hal?"

"No." There was no mistaking the anger in Brognola's voice, and it cut into the tension in the room.

"That means you're not operating with all the facts," Bolan went on. "For a man in your position, that's a pretty high risk."

Quartermain's voice hardened. "I don't want a bloodthirsty butcher roaming the streets of my city, endangering the lives of my citizens."

"That's where your problem begins, guy," the Executioner said in a graveyard voice, "because you've already got one, and he's dug in deep."

A nervous tic started under Quartermain's left eye. He started to put a hand to his face, caught himself, then put the hand away, averting his eyes a moment later from Bolan's unflinching gaze.

"This guy's playing all of us like a violin," Bolan went on, "and it's time you woke up to that. You've got people dying out there, people who are going down under bullets the man we're hunting for didn't fire. This isn't the time to be political or let a passion for momentary glory determine your course of action."

Quartermain erupted from the desk and threw a forefinger in the warrior's direction. "You're out of line, mister."

"And you're off track."

Quartermain spun on his heel to face Brognola. "This is the kind of attitude I was referring to, Brognola. I don't want this city turned into scorched earth or have to look at casualty lists and think of them as being within the limits of reasonable losses."

The big Fed tossed his soggy cigar in a wastepaper basket. "Let's cut the shit here, Counselor. This city's in trouble and this man can help."

"I don't want the kind of help he gave an hour ago."

Taking a step forward, Brognola lowered his voice and said, "Look, I'd rather work through you because you hold a certain number of ears in this town and can mold a large segment of the people involved here into a single unit. If it seems like you're going to stand in my way, I'll take the time to get you stepped on while we tend to business."

"You're bluffing."

"I never bluff."

Quartermain resumed his seat on the edge of the desk, the tic flaring to life again under his eye.

"You've got a lot of political pretensions, Quartermain," the big Fed said, "and a big ego for them to feed on. Now, you can either play ball with me, or I'll take your ass back with me in a briefcase when the dust settles on this thing."

"You can't do that."

"Sure I can. I've got a lot of friends on the Hill, Quartermain. Think about the ties to the Dallas situation, of who else may be backing Justice's interest in this." Brognola fell silent. "Then remember the time when you weren't such a successful lawyer or political image, to some of the cases where you weren't so selective about where your fees came from."

Quartermain started to say something, then caught himself. "I didn't do anything wrong. Those clients deserved representation."

"Yeah, but dredging up the past won't do your present or future career any good at all."

"That's blackmail."

"On the contrary," Brognola said, "that's politics. It's a dirty little business when you start playing in it, and you never really come clean again. Ask me how I know. The only good thing is that it provides a system that lets us get things done when dealing with the guys who want to wear the white hats at the expense of the guys who've been in muddy trenches for years."

Bolan studied Quartermain's face, seeing how the mind behind it worked, and grasped at the options left open. This was Brognola's game for the moment because he didn't have the leverage to move Quartermain. It also served to remind the warrior how he operated in the soldier's world, where black was black and white was white when there was fire in the hole. He was glad he didn't have to sort through all the grays that were Brognola's domain.

"Your decision," the big Fed prompted.

"Whatever happens," Quartermain said in a tight voice, "if anything goes wrong, it's on your head."

Brognola gave him a mirthless smile. "I was told that when I came down here, Quartermain, by someone I respect a whole lot more." He turned to Bolan. "You had a reason for dropping in?"

"Just a couple of ideas that may or may not pan out," the warrior said. "Quartermain, get some of your intelligence teams working on helicopter registrations for the birds that are in the air tonight. It's possible the team working this city has one or two units operational now for surveillance and drop zones."

"There are going to be a lot of them," Quartermain protested. "This is a business town. A lot of people fly in and out as necessary. There are a number of commercial craft as well as privately owned ones."

"Have them start with the privately owned ones," Bolan suggested. "Then get hold of the cellular telephone companies in the city and get crews working on installing mobile phones in the patrol cars."

Quartermain's confused expression showed he didn't understand. "Do you know how much money you're talking about?"

Bolan shook his head. "This isn't about money, guy, this is about establishing a communications link that won't be privy to outsiders listening in. I've watched the radio people catalog and monitor different frequencies since I've been here, and it's all been useless. That's because the man we're hunting knows cellular telephone transmissions are impossible to keep track of. Check the list of contents on that Volkswagen van. I did. It was equipped with a mobile telephone. He may not be using the frequencies, but you can bet his team is monitoring the police bands, just as the different media teams are. Their movement alone could cost you lives as things progress."

Quartermain reached for a phone on his desk.

"If you get the cellular phones installed, you can establish a private network for law enforcement to utilize. Then issue a blackout on the police bands, letting only regular calls feed through the frequency."

"That's going to take time," Quartermain said.

"That's why you should start now." Bolan glanced at Brognola, who couldn't conceal a small, satisfied grin. "If you need me, I'll be out there. You've got the number."

Brognola nodded, and the Executioner left, knowing the alliance with Quartermain and his troops was shaky at best, and eventually as dangerous as the war taking shape in Chicago's streets. He was alone, but it felt good to be moving again. Each step would take him closer to his quarry.

"YOU'RE THE ONE, aren't you?"

The parking area where Bolan had been forced to leave the Blazer was dimly lighted, making it hard to see the speaker.

She stepped from behind the big 4WD and took the glove off her right hand, leaving it ghostly pale in the night. She offered it to him.

Bolan stood his ground and ignored the hand, his combat senses rallying around his conscious mind as he checked for anyone who might be with her. "Have we met?"

The woman let the hand drop, then pulled her parka hood back. Black hair spilled out and framed an attractive face. "No, but maybe you've seen me. I'm Delaney Keller, a reporter for a local television station." She reached back and patted the Blazer. "I saw this on the footage my station ransomed off one of the camera crews lucky enough to have been at the bridge while the van was still blazing."

Bolan walked toward the door of his vehicle. "You wasted your time waiting out here," he said as he unlocked it. "The story's in there." He pointed at the police department.

Keller came up beside him and put her hand on the door. "I don't think so." Her voice was firm and uncompromising. "I think a lot of the real story is here, with you." She ran a hand along the body of the Blazer, letting her gloves slide over the bullet holes. "I have an excellent nose for news. It's what keeps me on the air when young women with sweet smiles approach the news director about my job.''

Climbing inside the Blazer, Bolan tried to shut the door only to find the woman standing in the way. "Short of handcuffing you for obstructing a federal agent in carrying out his duty and dropping you on your butt in the snow, Miss Keller, what can I do for you?''

She smiled up at him. "You're a man with a story. I want that story. In exchange, perhaps I'll be able to help you. Over the years, I've been able to build up a considerable pool of contacts and resources.''

"Not interested.''

"I'm not an easy person to be rid of.''

"I figured.''

"We could talk, just you and me. Like, what is it about you that would make you draw fire so quickly?''

Bolan reached down to the front of her parka and plucked at the almost invisible microphone peeping out of her zippered front. He kept pulling on it despite her protests, until the microcassette recorder tumbled free. He switched it off and gave it back to her. "Just you and me?" He turned the ignition and the big engine rumbled to life.

"I can help you on this," Keller said. "The same thing that happened in San Francisco and Dallas is happening here, isn't it?''

"No comment." Bolan cut the wheels and let off on the clutch, moving the Blazer onto the street with the newswoman clinging to the open door.

"Wait, dammit. You're making a mistake. Fox, damn you." Stumbling as she jogged through the hard-packed snow covering the street, Keller released the door.

Bolan shut it and glanced in the rearview mirror, catching sight of the woman as she climbed back up from the street. An on-coming car pinned her in its headlights and honked the horn. The gesture Keller made in response wasn't at all ladylike.

4

Snow continued to fall and seemed to drift in layers across the streets, rising high against curbs, parked cars and buildings. Mack Bolan stayed on the move, his war book lying open in the passenger seat of the Blazer as he worked down the list of possible hostages Aaron Kurtzman's computers had turned up, all people of wealth and power. During the past forty-five minutes, he'd confirmed police or private protection on three people and confirmed the fact that two others weren't at home.

He worked the steering wheel and the gear shift to pass the sporadic, slow-moving traffic, letting the action and the movement unwind the tension he felt. It took an effort of will to place himself in the unknown terrorist's mind. Thinking through his own wars had never taken on the aspect of hostages and including innocent people in the ante. The Executioner had always fought up close and personal, making sure it was the enemy he faced across his guns without bystanders being caught in the cross fire. Now there was no safe middle ground, and the enemy was operating away from its home territory as well. It would be hard to tumble to the operation by looking for patterns, because each effort would have to be individual, based on the latest city.

Frustration chafed at the soldier, as insistent as the falling snow. Experience told him he had no choice but to wait for the aggressor's next move. The problem was, his gut knew the next move would signal the beginning of the wholesale slaughter that had already taken place in the other cities.

He logged the time of the radio interference at 2:47 a.m. and automatically turned it up. The voice was harsh, and an unidentifiable accent lurked somewhere in the background, noticeable to Bolan only because of the time he'd spent in other countries. The reception was poor, broken intermittently by hums and buzzes, letting him know the speaker was using a beefed-up communications system to seize the frequency.

"Citizens of Chicago, you are already aware of our presence in your city through efforts made by your media people. What you don't know is the police force that is supposed to be defending you is working even harder to keep you in the dark about what is going on. There are federal teams of law-enforcement people within your city now, and they are striving just as hard to keep you ignorant of the present situation."

Bolan lifted the mobile phone and dialed the number Brognola had set up for his personal use at the police department. Remembered images of the atrocities committed in San Francisco and Dallas burned across the night shadows trapped in his windshield.

"There have already been deaths in your city," the voice went on. "The continuation of the violence is up to the various police departments, the people you depend on to protect your families. Law-enforcement officials in San Francisco and Dallas didn't listen to us. As a result, many people died who otherwise wouldn't have. Our deals have been made. The right people are willing to cooperate with us. If you want to prevent any more bloodshed in your streets, call your politicians. Get the police off the streets and away from us. They will listen if you force them to. Make them listen to you." There was a burst of crackling static, then the station returned to the air, filled with dead silence.

Bolan switched the radio off as Brognola answered at the other end.

"Striker?"

"Yes."

"You heard?"

"Yeah."

"Shit. All hell's breaking loose at this end. The goddamn switchboard's already lit up like a Christmas tree."

"They figured on that. With an announcement like that they're going to be able to put public pressure on every move the regular police make. They're also able to tie up the emergency phone numbers so if anyone does see or hear anything, they won't be able to get through. Did anyone get a fix on the station they used to broadcast from?"

"The communications people here are triangulating it now. It's probably a long shot."

Bolan navigated around a dump truck salting the icy streets.

"And you're right about the public pressure angle. Quartermain's ready to shit needles. You can bet it's going to roll downhill once word of this thing hits Wonderland. It won't take long before every move we make is so scrutinized that these bastards are going to know before we take the first step.''

"You got that right." Cold air filtered in through the random bullet holes spotting the Blazer's windshield and warred with the hot air blowing from the heater, but it was nowhere near the subzero knot that had formed in the warrior's stomach.

"Where are you now?" Brognola asked. His voice sounded distant and preoccupied.

"Going west on South Fifty-fifth Street, near Pulaski Road. I wanted to check some of the incoming traffic at Chicago Midway airport, then get a list of arrivals and departures scheduled for early tomorrow morning. With the weather the way it is, I opted for Midway or Meigs Field for a maverick pilot. Travis is covering Meigs. Most of the runway-clearing equipment is going to be concentrated on O'Hare, but someone private would be willing to take the chance of landing at either of those."

"Someone private or someone desperate," Brognola agreed. "You need to get turned around. The signal came from back east."

Bolan cut across the street and started gaining speed, threading through the loose traffic. He saw a patrol car come from a side street and cut in front of him, dirty slush spinning out from the tire chains and splashing across his windshield.

"They've got a fix on the signal," Brognola said. "It's still broadcasting over other frequencies."

The cold knot in Bolan's stomach hit bottom as the reality behind the big Fed's words hit home.

"You're going to have a lot of company when you hit the site," Brognola said. "So watch your ass."

Rolling down his window, Bolan clamped the magnetic base of the battery-operated cherry to the top of the Blazer and switched it on. He accelerated, muscling his way past the patrol car. "Where?"

"SOLDIER FIELD?" Sergeant Joe Trebeck looked away from the street to survey his partner. "Are they sure about that?"

Detective Jack Reid pulled the sliding gun rack from under the seat and lifted the 12-gauge riot shotgun free. "Yeah." His voice was grim, but a slight smile played on his lips. He opened the glove compartment and dumped a handful of double-aught shells into his pockets, adding more as he continued to speak. "If we catch the assholes there, Joey, you may get your chance to play in the big leagues after all."

Cutting back off Cermack Street, Trebeck shook his head. "These guys are pros, Jack. By the time we hit the stadium, they'll be history."

"Yeah, well, even if they haven't left, they're going to be history if we catch them." Reid canted the shotgun forward, then rolled his cuffs up to check the .32 revolver he habitually carried in an ankle holster.

The stadium swelled into view a few blocks later. At least half a dozen cruisers sat in the parking lot as Trebeck pulled to a stop. He studied the sports arena as he got out, snugging his coat in close to cut the chill wind.

Reid got out on the other side, the riot gun a hard bar in his hands. He was tall and lean, dressed in a turtleneck sweater with a letter jacket over that, jeans, black running shoes, and a watch cap pulled down low over the back of his neck. His face, almost bisected by the dirty-blond mustache that defied departmental regulations, was pinched and white in the cold.

Unsnapping the safety strap housing his Combat Magnum, Trebeck left the .357 in its holster and started forward, waving to one of the uniforms he recognized. He took the direct approach, toward the main gate. Reid walked along silently just behind him, the way he had for the past twelve years beginning in high school football. Trebeck held out a hand, and Reid put a walkie-talkie into it. Dropping it into a pocket as the uniform drew even with him, he asked, "We got anybody inside, Johnson?"

The man's voice was quiet, tense. "Not yet. We were waiting for your call."

The sergeant came to a stop at the perimeter gate. A heavy chain with an intimidating padlock barred the way, and barbed wire glinted evilly eight feet above them. He pulled on a pair of thin gloves that didn't really keep his hands warm but did keep his skin from freezing to metal and icy surfaces. He tugged on the chain, listened to the sharp tinkle of the links move, but the gate remained locked. He looked back up at the barbed wire. "What about security?"

Johnson shook his head. "We've tried the phone number the guard company had, but we didn't get an answer."

"What about vehicles? Are all the ones out here accounted for?"

"We're still running the plates."

Trebeck turned to Reid. "Lose the lock." He moved away to let his partner work on the padlock with a pick set.

"You think they're still inside?" Johnson asked.

Trebeck shrugged, trying to remember if the wind had felt this goddamned cold the last time he'd been out in it. The stadium's exterior wall was blank and desolate, a winter desert carved in stone and iron. He went over the layout in his mind, rebuilding his perspective from the times he and Reid had gone to see the Bears or the Sting play. Involuntarily he recalled the eyes of the FBI agent he'd muscled at Michigan Avenue Bridge. There had been a desolation there as well, colored volcanic blue. "The signal's still broadcasting, isn't it?"

"Yeah." Johnson turned up the collar on his coat and wrapped his arms across his chest.

"What about aerial support?"

"Got two birds in the air winging this way. Should be here in a matter of minutes."

"Radio them and tell them to hold back until I give the word." Trebeck scanned the upper tiers of the stadium. "Then get them switched over to Tach Two. We're going to run this thing ourselves."

"Might not be such a good idea."

Trebeck pinned the older man with his gaze.

"SWAT team's on its way. Frederickson's heading it up, and he wants to call the shots."

"Screw Fredrickson," Reid called as he stepped back from the gate with the padlock in one hand. He dropped the lock to one side and smiled.

Looking back up at the stadium, Trebeck curbed his anger and asked, "What's SWAT's ETA?"

"In this weather, fifteen or twenty minutes. It's hard to say."

"That's too long." Trebeck waved toward the cruisers. "Those cars aren't exactly invisible out here, and these guys aren't dummies. They know the broadcast is being traced. We're going in."

Johnson smiled. "I was kind of hoping you'd see it that way, Joe." He trotted back to his car.

Reid took right point after they pushed the gate open, struggling against the dirty snow that piled up behind it. Trebeck carried the Combat Magnum in one hand, the walkie-talkie in the other. "I want two cars inside," he ordered. "The rest of you I want on foot."

A chorus of acknowledgments broke up the static.

"Johnson, I want you in one of the cars. If anything goes down wrong, you're in charge until Frederickson arrives."

"Yes, sir."

"If an unidentified vehicle arrives while we're inside, I want it put down. Take no chances. And keep running those plates through Dispatch."

"Yes, sir."

Trebeck's feet felt stiff with the cold as he moved toward the shadows hugging the stadium. He checked over his shoulder as the two cruisers he'd called for rocked across the frozen snow without lights. Eleven men formed two lines on either side of the vehicles. He stopped for a moment, waved them to spread out farther, then trailed his partner.

Reid took one side of the entrance as he took the other. Trebeck stared into the dark gathered on the other side of the glass door.

"See anything?" Reid asked.

"No."

"Since I'm the junior partner, I'll try the door." He wore a sarcastic grin.

"You just watch your ass, Jack. I've still got to take you back to your Mom in the morning." Trebeck raised the .357 as he extended his arm around the corner.

Reid stayed with the wall and the shadows until he reached the doors. He tugged, and the door swung outward easily. Scooping up snow with his foot, he made an ice doorstop and moved inside. Once he secured the hall, he waved.

Trebeck followed, choosing to keep his force intact rather than chance using men who'd never been fired on to search other areas. He kept the Combat Magnum pointed straight up at shoulder level, ready to drop it into target acquisition at a second's notice. The radio squawked in his hand as dark outlines of snack stands came into view. "Go," he whispered.

"Trebeck, this is Zimmer."

Recognizing the helicopter pilot's name, Trebeck said, "What is it?"

"Why don't you let us come in? We could hit the field and seats with the high-density spots and make sure you guys aren't walking into some kind of setup."

"Negative, Zimmer. If these people are still here and unaware of us, your arrival will have the same effect on them as roaches getting caught when the lights go on. I don't want them scurrying everywhere. We're going to do this nice and neat, all in one bundle."

"Roger. Clear."

"I want radio silence on this channel," Trebeck went on, letting some of the irritation he felt at the interruption show, "until we have something concrete. Trebeck clear." He waved to his partner and they moved forward, closing in on the first security light.

The interior was warmer than outside, and the absence of the wind made it seem even more so. Trebeck felt perspiration gather at the top of his spine and run down inside his clothes. He wanted to take the coat off but knew the light gray color of his sweatshirt would make him stand out in the night. He pocketed the walkie-talkie as he closed on his partner.

Reid reached the exit overlooking the seats at the home end zone and remained flat against the wall as he used the barrel of the riot gun to break the light overhead. Glass tinkled against the floor in the sudden darkness.

Hunkering beside his partner, Trebeck stared out across the rows of empty seats, aware that there were too many hiding places in front of them. A chill climbed his spine as he remembered the weapons the FBI agent had in the Blazer. Most of the gear had been equipped with night sights.

"We've been made," Reid whispered hoarsely. He tapped the glass door above him.

Trebeck looked up, spotting the foggy spot on the glass.

Reid trailed a finger through it. "On the outside." He looked at Trebeck. "Bastards made us coming in. It's your call, Joe."

Trebeck widened his eyes, willing his night vision to clear. Nothing moved out on the field. He wiped his chin with the back of his hand. "You feel lucky?"

"Every day of my life." Reid grinned.

"Hope you're right." Trebeck pushed a door open. "We're going to go, me and you, and we'll call it from up front."

"Seats on the fifty-yard line? Sounds good to me."

"These guys have probably got sniper scopes and shit, so they've got a better chance of seeing us before we see them."

"You wearing your vest tonight?"

"Yeah."

"So am I. So what are we waiting for? Let's paint a big red *S* on our chest and move on this."

"You ever heard of armor-piercing bullets?"

Reid smiled again and duck-walked out into the winter wind, the shotgun held chest-high over his knees. Trebeck waved to the uniformed policemen behind him, then followed.

Eerie shadows hugged the seats, turned them into markers for forbidden territory. Trebeck tried to maintain a loose grip on the .357 to dry out the perspiration staining the insides of his gloves. A familiar scent tinted the air, tugging playfully at his memory. The wind was a blasting furnace of icy coals that slid rigid pokers through his clothing. Snow covered the field, erasing all of the lines, making the goalposts at the visitor's end zone look like the horns of some buried beast.

He glanced over at Reid, saw that the man was already four rows farther down than he was. He picked up speed, using his empty hand to aid his descent across the ice-slick steps. The cold blurred his vision and made sustained staring impossible. To the left, high up in the seats, were the communications rooms set up for media coverage of the games. If the people responsible for the frequency theft were still broadcasting, they had to be in one of those rooms.

"Joe!"

Trebeck squinted, having difficulty finding Reid at first. His partner was pointing toward the goalposts in the home end zone. Nausea tightened his stomach when he saw the dark shapes suspended from the crossbar a yard or more from the ground. He slipped on the steps and slid painfully across a half-dozen sharp corners before he caught himself. By then his partner was in full motion, slithering through the seats on his belly while angling for the wall directly behind the goalpost. Trebeck eased the hammer back on the .357 and followed, feeling blood trickle down one leg.

"Jack, back off," Trebeck called.

Reid came to a stop at the wall.

Trebeck skidded into place beside his partner.

Three bodies, two of them women, hung lifelessly from the crossbar, twisting slightly in the wind. The shrill shriek of metal whispered into Trebeck's ears, raising the hair on his neck. The unidentified odor touched him again, logging into his mind, bringing images of the other deaths he'd seen.

"I saw one of them move."

"They're dead, Jack." Trebeck made his voice harsh so he'd believe what he said as well.

"Son of a bitch," Reid cursed. He looked at Trebeck. "We can't just leave them there."

Trebeck scanned the field, not sure what he was even supposed to be looking for.

The three bodies swung again, followed immediately by the scratching sound of metal on metal. Trebeck studied them for independent movement, willing himself to see some signs of life if there were any. It was too dark to be sure. Unwilling to stand by if there was a chance, he threw an arm over the wall and pulled himself across.

His feet shushed into the snowdrifts below, chilling him almost up to his groin. He felt exposed at once, naked and vulnerable, like the kid he'd been when he and Jack Reid had tramped through the old neighborhood trying to stay clear of the wrong gangs.

Reid thumped into the drift beside him.

Aware of the heated perspiration gathering inside his clothing, Trebeck legged through the drifts, breaking ground toward the goalpost.

He touched the first body, feeling the cold slackness of it, feeling the icy film that had already formed in the clothing. The woman's face was a pale oval above a throat slit ear to ear, suspended by wire that was pulled through the gash so tight it looked like the corpse hung by the spine alone.

"Sweet Jesus," Reid breathed as he checked the person at the opposite end of the crossbar. Long wisps of gray fog trailed from his mouth as he spoke.

Trebeck started to wave him back to the safety of the wall, but the flat crack of a high-powered weapon splintered the deadly quiet inside the stadium. It was followed by another and another, less than a heartbeat apart. Trebeck watched a body plummet from one of the overhead camera platforms and disappear into a snowdrift. Another body tumbled after it as the night evaporated when the field lights were abruptly switched on. The reflected glare from the snow was blinding. He spun toward Reid, reaching for him as autofire shuddered to life around him.

Something crunched between his shoulder blades and punched him to the ground.

THE EXECUTIONER reloaded the sniping rifle and chambered the first round as he sighted through the Zeiss Diavari D telescopic sight. Muzzle-flashes marked the position, the scope made it personal, bringing the sniper's head and shoulders into focus. His finger caressed the trigger as the cross hairs settled over the man's vulnerable neck. The 7.62 mm round caught the man, mushrooming on impact, and hurled him from the camera mount.

Bolan worked the bolt action without waiting to see where the body dropped. There was a lot of movement below, but so far he had an open attack zone because the police team hadn't begun their assault. A withering barrage of fire from at least three positions chewed away the tops of the seats above him.

Marking them in his mind, the warrior shifted and quick-footed his way down the steep stairs leading to the top rows of the stadium.

He saw Trebeck go down suddenly as the field lights were switched on, followed by his partner a moment later. The warrior got set up behind another row of seats as autofire raked the immediate area. Night had turned to day under the high-intensity lights, making concealment even more difficult. Something caught at his watch cap and burned through his hair. He squeezed the trigger, rode out the heavy-calibered weapon's recoil and moved on to his next target.

Shot number two smashed through the glass window of the announcer's booth, catching a man in the chest. Bolan worked the bolt, pumped the next round through the unmasked face. He glanced at Trebeck lying motionless in the snow, knowing there was too much distance separating them to entertain thoughts of attempting a rescue if the man wasn't already dead. Bolan had kicked the play into action, hoping to draw the attention of the snipers with the two undercover detectives in their sights. Professionalism had kept them on target.

And it was that same kind of professionalism that was needed to keep the cross fire from turning into a bloodbath, Bolan reminded himself as he thumbed more cartridges into his weapon. Running footsteps shushed at him through the snow, alerting him to the presence of an enemy. He turned to see a Kevlar-armored attacker swing around the end of the row of seats with an Uzi gripped in both gloved hands.

Bolan shoved himself to his feet, leaped and skidded painfully against the seats two rows up as he sought new cover. Splinters and padding flew in all directions as bullets exploded into the seats. He felt warmth spread along the right side of his chest as he crawled along the maze of steel chair legs. He drew the Desert Eagle after slinging the FN, came to a halt ten feet farther along the row, waited until the gunner showed himself, then triggered a 240-grain round that caught the nose bridge of the Kevlar mask and crumpled it inward. Another round smashed through the revealed jawline and sent the body tumbling down the steps.

Autofire tracked the falling corpse.

Breath streaming out in gray clouds, Bolan holstered the .44 and shoved his way into the open again. Shadows weaved through the sepia darkness created by the floodlights out on the field, interspersed by bright muzzle-flashes.

Uniformed policemen filled the area above the home end zone where Trebeck and his partner had gone down, but with pistols and riot guns they weren't successful in returning fire. Sniper fire chewed their ranks to bits as the brief rally became a massacre. The survivors quickly took refuge wherever they could find it. Bodies hung draped over the railings and littered the white snow.

The Executioner unslung his rifle as he took cover behind a flight of stone steps. He fitted the scope to his eye and the stock to his shoulder as he leaned into his field of fire. The cross hairs swam dizzily against the backdrop of stadium seats, centering on the exposed forearm of one man. The warrior released a half breath, caressed the trigger, rode out the recoil and caught his target again as the man turned and ran. He put the cross hairs over the back of the man's neck, breathed out, squeezed again. The bullet hit the terrorist near the base of the skull, shoved him forward as if he'd been poleaxed, then let him spill lifelessly to the steps.

Sparks splintered from the stone steps as autofire converged on the Executioner's new position. He shifted, hunkered down and picked his next target. Centering his next shot on the back of a seat where one of the gunners was hiding, he squeezed, worked the bolt again and put the fourth shot an inch lower than the first. There was no return fire from that position.

Movement in the announcer's booth drew his attention as he ducked back down to reload the rifle. Lights flashed on the glass from equipment that was in use inside. Cold anticipation crept up his spine as he guessed what the booth was being used for, making him realize the strike team waiting for the police team was designed to do more than introduce law-enforcement people to the kind of firepower they were up against.

He peeled a fragmentation grenade from his combat harness, stepped into the open for an instant and lobbed it toward the booth. Autofire sought him out, burning under the snow across the concrete. A moment later the front of the booth exploded. The Beretta 93-R in hand, he trotted forward four rows, then came up with it in a Weaver's stance as he searched for survivors.

The grenade hadn't done as much damage as he'd hoped. The large glass had been blown away with most of one corner of the building, and spot fires had caught in the electrical systems. The back door swung emptily.

Shadows ran across the white expanse of the football field.

At first Bolan thought it was a ground attack aimed at bagging the rest of Trebeck's forces, then he noticed the way they split up into twos and each made for a corpse. He shouldered his rifle. The range was a little over a hundred yards, not a difficult shot for a man-size target, but it was complicated by the differing light levels and the Kevlar armor.

The Executioner's first round knocked his target down, forcing the guy to let go of the corpse. Seconds later, the man was back up, still intent on removing the body. Dark stains followed in the snow as the teams made for the locker rooms and exits at that end.

Autofire raked Bolan's position, pinning him under the sudden thunder. He didn't hear the sound of the helicopters until they were almost directly overhead. For a moment the roving spotlights captured him, then he was diving headlong an instant before friendly fire reached out for him.

He rolled from the steps, dropping painfully, taking refuge in one of the corridors leading back through the stadium, cutting him off from the action. The helicopters passed by with the familiar *whup whup whup* of the blades beating air. Knowing what would surely happen, aware that aerial retaliation had to have been allowed for, he hurled himself back up the ramp.

As he regained a clear view of the battle zone, a small comet arced toward the lead helicopter, transforming it into an orange-and-yellow fireball that roiled up into the sky, spitting out bits and pieces of the metal skeleton.

5

Forcing himself to his feet despite the fear that gripped him and the pain burning between his shoulder blades, Trebeck searched for his partner. "Get up, Jack!" His voice was harsh, raspy, and there wasn't enough air in his lungs. The bulletproof vest under his coat and sweatshirt had prevented penetration, but the impact had been more hellish than he'd thought possible.

He stumbled through the snowdrift, back through the hanging bodies swaying in the wind, and reached for Reid. Fisting his partner's coat, he tugged, flipping the body over. Scarlet stained the whiteness, becoming two-dimensional black eating into the satin brilliance the field lights had created. A puckered crater on one side of Reid's head led to the gaping hole where the round had exploded through.

Nausea gripped Trebeck. He forced it down, letting Reid's body gently roll back facedown.

Bullets kicked powdery puffs loose from the snow and drove him to shelter as at least one round tugged at the hem of his coat.

He made his mind work, tried to devise some strategy to salvage the situation. The whole thing had been a suck play from beginning to end. The broadcast, the way Dispatch had been able to triangulate the position, and the bodies of the hostages waiting for them. He hunkered down behind the goalpost because he knew he'd be an easy mark for the unseen snipers if he tried to run across the field. The walkie-talkie was gone from his pocket, lost somewhere in the snow.

He glared toward the area where he'd judged the initial sniper fire to have originated. Movement high among the seats alerted him, and he followed it until he made out the man in black still laying down a field of fire. A moment later the man threw something, then the announcer's booth exploded and became wreathed in flames. He knew at once who the man was.

Even as he started to move out, another blast of autofire raked the seats at the home end. Trebeck glanced up, suddenly aware of the screams above him. Bodies of the uniformed policemen who'd followed him into the stadium were spilled haphazardly across the seats and railings. As he watched, two men slid free of the crossbars and tumbled to the field. The way they hit and remained motionless let Trebeck know his partner wouldn't be the only casualty the PD suffered tonight.

Peering around the goalpost, he saw the terrorists come from the opposite end of the field to retrieve the fallen bodies of their comrades. Trebeck threw himself prone as bullets smashed into the goalpost near his head, torn between losing the FBI agent in the darkness and trying to stop the attack force. He leveled the Combat Magnum, taking time to squeeze the rounds off single-action to make sure of his aim, aiming for what he hoped would be vulnerable points of the body armor.

He rolled over on his back as he emptied the brass and reached for one of the three speed-loaders he carried. There was no doubt in his mind that Fox was responsible in part for Reid's death. If the guy had been onto the suck that early, he could have put a call through, or intercepted them before they became committed. He rolled over again, moving outward from the goalpost, judging from the activity at the other end of the field that neither his nor Fox's bullets had done anything about cutting down the odds.

The sound of the helicopter rotors filled his ears, drowning out the sound of his own racing heart. He glanced up, tracking them across the sky, blinking against the swirl of falling snow.

With the lights winking, the tail sections clearly marked Police in black on white, Trebeck was suddenly aware of what good targets they made. He pushed himself to his feet, heading for Reid's body and the walkie-talkie the other man had carried.

A flare lighted up the landscape around him, followed by the crack of the explosion, then the concussive force and heat that buffeted him to the ground.

Trebeck came up spluttering, hand still tight around his weapon, and saw the wreckage of the lead helicopter even as the second turned into a fireball a heartbeat later. The second explosion caught him more prepared, causing him to cover his head as metal and fiberglass rained down around him.

Fire and smoke curled up from the wreckage scattered over the field and the seats. Sucking in the cold and metallic taste of the whipping winds, Trebeck staggered to his feet, made his way to Reid's body and lifted the walkie-talkie the man had carried. He squatted, leaning against the wall as he keyed it to life and called for the SWAT commander.

The seats and field were empty of living shadows. Trebeck ran his gun hand along his forehead, surprised to see blood smeared from his knuckles to his wrist.

Fredrickson, the SWAT commander, was harsh and brutal in his reply. "Got yourself into one hell of a fucking mess, didn't you, Trebeck? Had to be Johnny Hero. Christ, I got spotters on the wall telling me you're littered with dead."

"We don't have time for this shit, Fredrickson."

"You're goddamn right we don't, thanks to you. This wasn't a goddamn beachhead you were supposed to Rambo your way through. The only two helicopters we had in the area you got shot to shit."

"Did your spotters tell you the guys we're after are busy legging it out the visitors' end?" Radio static was the only reply. Trebeck used his elbows to regain his feet. The .357 felt like an anvil at the end of his arm, too heavy to pull up again if he had to. His vision swam, blurred by the blood leaking down into his eyes and the high-intensity floodlights. "You got a Feeb in here, too, Fredrickson."

"Who?"

"Guy named Fox. Ran into him down at the bridge on Michigan Avenue. He's connected pretty heavy."

"Son of a bitch'll have to look out for his own ass. What's he doing here?"

"I want to know the answer to that one myself. He opened this little shindig instead of warning us about the setup."

"You saying he used your team for bait?"

"I'm saying I want to look him in the eye myself when he answers the question." Trebeck pocketed the walkie-talkie and found the strength to keep going. He worked a stumbling trot into a run, rolled over the top of the wall at the foot of the area where he'd seen the FBI agent vanish, then headed for the quickest gate that would let him into the outside perimeters. Even if the attackers got away, he wanted Fox, and he wanted the man in the worst way. He tightened his grip on the .357.

THE EXECUTIONER was in motion as the second helicopter smashed onto the football field. He slung his rifle over his shoulder and drew the Desert Eagle, charging the automatic with a fresh magazine. The numbers were running low on the strike for all of them now, leaving everything to be done on the heartbeat, and shouldering the sniping weapon would slow down his reaction time.

Turning into the first walkway he found, Bolan cut toward the upper tiers of seats. The howling sirens in the background were captured and magnified inside the stadium. There were no bodies left on the field. The recovery mission had been a success. He urged himself to greater speed, realizing his only chance of penetrating the mystery surrounding the strike force was in getting his hands on one of the bodies and letting Kurtzman's computers do their thing.

He peered through the snowy darkness overlaying the parking area. The men came through the bottom gate at a full run, bodies slung haphazardly between two to four men. At least twenty men fanned out with the corpses and the wounded as three black Volkswagens broke through the red-and-white-striped barricades and chain fences enclosing the parking area.

Bolan pulled his collapsible grappling hook from one of the pockets of the skinsuit and secured it around the top railing. Leathering the .44, he stepped over the side, played out the slack in the thin nylon cord, then began rappeling down the concrete sides of the stadium.

A siren changed decibels, becoming clearer. Spinning red-and-white lights revolved over the snow in the parking area as a large SWAT truck barreled into view, followed by three patrol cruisers. Spotlights mounted beside the doors flashed, targeting immediately on the three vans skidding to a stop in front of the waiting group.

The SWAT truck smashed through the snowdrifts even though autofire raked its sides. One of the patrol cruisers spun out of control, its windshield shattered and torn away by the volley of 5.56 mm tumblers that reached through and killed the driver.

Halfway down the stadium wall, one of the spotlights touched Bolan, alerting police teams and his quarry to his presence. Concrete chips exploded and spun from the wall above and below him. At least two rounds thudded painfully into his Second Chance armor. He let the cord pay out more quickly, working to keep his body closer to the wall. His hands burned. Something caught the cord, whipping it to one side, then the pressure went away as gravity snatched the Executioner's body. As he plummeted to the ground he realized a bullet had cut the cord. There was time to slide the sniper rifle from his shoulder, then he willed himself to go limp, hoping the snowdrift below was deep enough.

Whiteness closed over him, burning his face with the cold, muffling the recognizable chatter of the M-60s that had just kicked into life. The sudden stop hurt, and knocked the breath from his lungs.

The Executioner fanned off the layers of snow as he rolled to his left, toward the vans, and drew the Desert Eagle. The barrel of the .44 raised to target acquisition as he sighted on the nearest bipod-mounted M-60 in the belly of a van. He burned through the clip, catching the gunner with one of the early rounds and shoving him against the opposite side of the Volkswagen.

The SWAT truck's nose suddenly erupted in flames as a warhead from a rocket launcher exploded into it. Men in dark uniforms spilled from the back, silhouetted against the torn field of snow. Daisy chains from the M-60s tore the life from some of them before they could take cover.

Bolan could smell the destruction as he reached into a canvas bag at his waist. The SWAT truck blew without warning, ripping apart from the inside as weapons and armament went up as well. He threw his grenade, ducking into the drift again as 7.62 mm rounds vectored in on his position. The van he'd aimed for threw slush from its tires as the grenade went off behind it, blowing out the rear windows. The vehicles bore no license plates, and they kept their lights off as they sped off toward the side street they'd entered on.

Standing up, Bolan found that the two cruisers that had survived the onslaught more or less intact had wallowed to stops in the waist-high drifts. His body felt the cold, but it would never touch the anger trapped inside him. He fed a new magazine into the .44 and released the slide to snap back into place. The sound was grim, cutting through the cacophony of police noises behind him.

"Hold it right there, asshole!" a man yelled.

Bolan turned slowly, lifting his hands.

The man came forward, flanked by three others, carrying a long-handled flashlight. Behind them, bodies from the SWAT team lay like dead shadows.

"I'm Fox," Bolan said as they closed in on him, "with the FBI."

"I'll be a raped ape," one of the men said vehemently as he put his revolver away.

Bolan recognized the man as one of the officers who'd covered the incident at the bridge.

"Put your pieces away, guys," the patrolman said. "He's who he says he is." His glare was hard and piercing.

The Executioner holstered the Desert Eagle. "Did anyone follow those vans?"

The cop shook his head. More men, on foot, came around the curve of the stadium.

Feeling the cold now despite the insulation of the skinsuit and the Second Chance armor, Bolan left the group forming around the flaming SWAT truck and headed toward the Blazer.

"Fox!"

Bolan turned at the sound of his assumed name, seeing Trebeck's angry face for an instant above the right cross that hammered into his chin and sent him sprawling backward.

"YOU'RE A MADMAN," the mayor of Chicago said in a voice filled with quiet desperation.

Wearing his mask again, Dreyse studied the man in grim silence. Then he smiled a cold, cruel smile. Standing on the open deck of the yacht with Lake Michigan spread around them, he knew he was lost against the backdrop of night.

The mayor stood before him, framed in the subtle light of the doorway leading down into the yacht. He held his shoulders in his own hands, shivering with fear and from the cold. Over pastel-green pajamas he wore an expensive jacket that offered more prestige than warmth. He was barefoot. As Dreyse watched, the man's toes curled and uncurled involuntarily. "You're not going to get away with this," the mayor said.

Dreyse shook his head, as if talking to a child. "Yes, I will. I already have. The only thing that remains is to exact my price for returning this city to its citizens. And that will come with the morning and the opening of the banks."

"My wife is having a breakdown in there, dammit. You can't keep her here."

"What would you suggest?"

"Let her go."

"So she could tell authorities where to find us?" Dreyse shook his head. "I don't think so." He held up a hand to silence the man. "Alive is better than dead. She'll make it through the night, just as we all will. If you wish, I can have a bottle of brandy brought to you, to calm her."

"You can't expect to hold a whole city hostage like this. No one will stand for it."

Dreyse let the cruel smile touch his lips again. "Standing or sitting, it doesn't matter one whit. This country has had it good far too long. The U.S. has freely plundered in other, less fortunate, countries and suffered no real punitive damage. It has carried out terrorist activities, all with the unknowing blessing of the American people. Those villainies have returned home to roost."

The mayor squinted at him in the darkness, smoothing his thinning hair back. "Is that what this is about? Politics?"

Dreyse laughed. "Hardly. This is about money. Politics is a useful lever to find fortune at times, though slowly. But this isn't one of those times. I have a goal, one that I intend to meet, and the means is the knowledge I have acquired in different areas of the globe. I know how to fight, and I know how to kill, and I have found those skills to be very marketable in the past. Now that I have gone into business for myself, I still find them useful."

The mayor stared at him, eyes bulging in disbelief.

"This is the land of the fatted cow," Dreyse went on. "The modern United States of America has never had a war within its borders, never had to watch its citizens fight and die in the streets, never had to burn corpses or bury them in community pits to keep disease and pestilence at a minimum. Terrorism is a term they have all come to know, but they've never known it face-to-face. Hostages were always people who were in the wrong country at the wrong time. Even then there were those who were willing to liberate large sums of money to free friends and relatives in foreign countries. Remember the MIAs of Vietnam? There's still talk among the people to ransom missing soldiers back." He narrowed his gaze and lowered his voice. "It's time the people of this country saw terrorism in its realest form."

"But why?"

"For the money." Dreyse shrugged. "Contrary to your opinion, we aren't madmen, nor are we pursuing a hopeless quest for balancing some nonexistent scales. We are here because the trade we have to offer will flourish. At least for a time."

"And during that time you'll keep on killing?"

"Every salesman has to make a demonstration, Mr. Mayor. You've been a businessman long enough to understand that."

"They've been waiting for you," the mayor said, "ever since Dallas and San Francisco. You can bet your ass that right now Chicago is crawling with federal authorities who aren't going to walk away until they crucify you."

"Let them try." Dreyse turned away from the man, facing toward the captive city. The skyline was almost drowned by the falling snow. Tall buildings looked gray against the night, filled with lighted windows that made them look even larger. "I didn't come here to fail. Now, you should be getting back below. Your continued absence will make your wife worry even more, and exposure to the cold won't be healthy. It would be ridiculous for you to live through this situation only to die of pneumonia."

The mayor left, the unblemished rectangle of light returning to the deck to mark his departure.

"Vogelsang?"

"Sir?"

"Have a closer watch maintained on our guests until this plays out."

"Yes, sir."

Dreyse took off his mask and walked to the prow of the yacht where he'd had the mobile telephone installed when the vessel had been taken over earlier in the evening. He relished the cold, even the dry cold of North America, because it reminded him of home.

An orange flare went up to the west.

Pulling a pair of binoculars from inside his coat, Dreyse focused on the area, marking it as Soldier Field. Another orange flare followed immediately, the field glasses pulling enough of it in to identify it as an explosion. He watched the color fade from the night.

Minutes later the phone rang.

"Yes," he said.

"It has been done," Moltke stated.

"And the difficulties?"

"A little more than we had expected."

"Why?"

"The man from the bridge incident was there."

Dreyse considered it. "Put someone on him. I want to know who he is before he gets to be more of a problem."

"Yes, sir."

"What of the tapes?"

"They were taken."

Dreyse allowed himself to smile because no one would see it. "Good, Karl, very good. Have the second unit begin their attack. Even this mystery man can't be in two places at once. And make sure they take film of the assault. I want copies of both distributed to the television stations on your list."

"Yes, sir." Moltke broke the connection.

Dreyse refocused the binoculars, pointing them toward the Chicago police headquarters, thinking how pleasant it was that a set of plans could roll along so well even if there did appear to be a fly in the ointment. He waited patiently.

"YOU SON OF A BITCH."

Bolan blocked Trebeck's next blow, catching the inside of the man's swing on his forearm as he tried to regain his footing in the treacherous snow. There was enough force behind it to keep him off balance and floundering in the drift. Disabling the man would have been easy; taking him down without permanent injury was a different matter.

The detective's face was twisted into a mask of fury, letting Bolan know at once that the man's partner hadn't made it through the cross fire. Trebeck kicked out, his big foot seeming to whistle out of nowhere from under cover of his coat.

Catching the detective's foot in his hands, Bolan twisted, letting go before bones broke as he shoved his opponent away. He pushed himself to his feet, sliding the sniper rifle's sling from his shoulder as he watched Trebeck lurch back to a standing position.

The snow was colored with the flashing lights and fires streaming from the burning SWAT van. A circle of uncertain policemen closed in around them.

"You goddamn bastard!" Trebeck roared. "You knew there was a trap waiting for us inside the stadium. Do you know how many men are dead because of the little game you played here?"

Bolan stepped inside the detective's attack as the man closed again, hearing Trebeck's breath whistle in his ear as he drove home a short right to the man's abdomen. Trebeck seemed to deflate for a moment. "There wasn't a damn thing I could have done," Bolan growled. He kept his hand on the man's neck, forcing him to remain subdued. "By the time I got here your people were already inside."

Jerking away, Trebeck came up swinging. He jabbed and feinted, getting through Bolan's defenses with a fist that split the inside of the Executioner's lower lip.

Bolan tasted blood as he stepped back. He had to check his movements to keep from landing a crippling blow. Most of the fights the warrior was involved in were to the death, not against someone on the same side. When Trebeck came in again, he tagged the man with a left that jarred the guy and sent him stumbling backward.

The detective shook his head to clear it.

Low voices gained in intensity as more law-enforcement people crowded around. Bolan realized the fight with Trebeck wasn't the only one he'd have on his hands if he tried to leave.

"If it wasn't for you," Trebeck said as he wiped at the blood trickling down his chin, "Jack would still be alive. You let us walk into that ambush, used us for bait while you picked off a few guys." He swung a hard right.

Bolan dodged easily, falling into a matching orbit with the left hook Trebeck brought in from nowhere. He swung and was blocked immediately, feeling the punishing power the detective had in his long arms as

Trebeck hammered him with a blow to the rib cage. His breath whooshed out of him at once despite the Kevlar vest.

"Did you bag enough guys to satisfy you, Fox?" Trebeck asked as he waded in again. Scarlet threads twisted through his white teeth.

Rocking the man with another solid left to the jaw instead of the throat, Bolan caught one of Trebeck's flailing fists, twisted the wrist to bring it up behind the man's back, then launched the detective facedown into the snowdrift. He took a deep breath that shuddered through his bruised rib cage. The man could hit. "The problem is that you people haven't taken this team seriously enough," Bolan said in a voice loud enough to be heard by the crowd of policemen. "These guys are trained strike teams, and they're damn sure not striking blind."

Trebeck lurched to his feet and swayed for a moment.

"Everything they've done so far has been carefully calculated for the effect they want." Bolan lifted his arms to defend himself again. "If I'd radioed in what I thought, it would have only started the bloodshed earlier, and that's if I'd been taken seriously. The mobile phones I'd advised Quartermain to get installed would have helped."

"You're talking like this is a goddamn war," one of the policemen called.

Bolan faced the crowd. "It is. Don't believe for a second that it isn't. This team has already penetrated your defenses without being identified, and even the right way of extracting them is going to cost lives. They wanted to leave a message for you people when they set this up, and they wanted to leave one for the people who live in this city. They didn't hesitate about carving it into the body of every person they killed back there. They won't hesitate about using any of you as an example." He looked back at Trebeck. "I'm sorry about your partner, but if you people don't wake up to what it is you're facing here, there are going to be a lot more dead cops and hostages."

"You're full of shit, Fox," Trebeck retorted. He pointed at the stadium. "Those people aren't going to take the type of action you handed back to them lying down. They're going to retaliate." He wiped at the blood still dribbling from his nose. "And they'll probably retaliate by killing even more hostages."

Bolan didn't say anything. The stares of the assembled group of policemen were full of stark menace. Even if he could convince them of the kind of people they were up against, they'd never accept him as one of their own.

Reaching behind his back, Trebeck brought out a pair of gleaming handcuffs. "Cooperation be damned," he said as he started forward. "You're a fucking menace to society while you're running around. Way I see it, we can find some place to stash you and handle this situation without the body count going up faster than inflation."

Knowing if he made a move to draw a weapon he'd probably be gunned down, Bolan stood his ground. His fight, even back in the Mafia days, had never been with the law-enforcement people, and he'd made it an unwritten code that he'd never draw on a badge.

"This should make a good story," a feminine voice said as Trebeck reached for Bolan's arm.

Heads turned, and the detective froze.

A Minicam whirred to life on top of a man's shoulder. Beside him, framed in silhouette against the light from the camera, a smaller shadow stepped forward.

Bolan recognized her at once as the news reporter who'd accosted him in front of the Chicago police headquarters. Her face was centered in the hood of a parka, and a small smile twisted her lips.

"What the hell are you doing here, Delaney?" A rugged man in slacks and trench coat stepped forward with his hands in his pockets and a harsh look on his hawk-nosed face. "This area's restricted."

"You should tell the guys back there, Murchison," Delaney Keller said. She moved forward, having trouble maneuvering through the snowdrifts.

"Pack your camera and move it along," Murchison growled. "You newspeople will be given the scoop when the liaison guys arrive."

Keller shook her head. "You expect me to wait for the watered-down version of what happened here?"

Murchison confronted her. "I'm not giving you a choice."

"There's that little matter of freedom of the press, remember?" Keller looked up at him.

Murchison remained silent. The Minicam whirred away, the cameraman shifting the bright lights across every detail within reach. Bolan noticed how the handcuffs disappeared in Trebeck's big hand.

"I can hold off the inside story for a while," Keller said, "and I figure that's being pretty damned generous since Eric and I have already done some footage inside the stadium while you big macho guys have been wrestling around out here in the snow."

Murchison's face remained impassive. "What do you want?"

Keller's smile was sweet. "An interview, of course."

Murchison shook his head. "Can't give you that till the PR guys get here, Delaney. You know the routine."

"I thought I might get one from the federal team involved in this."

Throwing a finger in Bolan's direction, Murchison said, "That son of a bitch isn't going anywhere, much less take time out to give you a statement."

Keller took a microphone from her pocket. "Care to tell the people why, Captain Murchison?"

"Get that thing out of my face."

"Give me the interview."

"Hell, no. You're interfering in police business. Clear the area, or we're taking you into custody, too."

"Why are you arresting Special Agent Fox?" Keller pressed.

"I don't have to tell you a damn thing."

Ignoring the statement, Keller shoved the microphone forward again. "Why was Sergeant Trebeck fighting Special Agent Fox?"

"They weren't fighting." Murchison pushed the microphone away.

"That's what I'd call it."

"Well, you'd be calling it wrong."

"Eric got some of it on tape. We can let the audience be the judge."

Murchison pointed at two men. "Confiscate that camera."

"Police business, Captain," Keller asked, "or are you trying to cover up something?"

"Blow it out your ass, Delaney."

The two policemen started forward. The cameraman kept filming.

"It's your choice," the reporter said. "That camera is wired to the station, and they've been taping everything we've seen since coming here. If you want to start playing hardass, you and this whole goddamn posse of yours will be on the tube in five minutes. Unless you intend to confiscate the television station as well."

Murchison glared at her. "What's the deal, Delaney? We've known each other for years and you've never tried to pull any shit like this."

"The stakes weren't as high."

Waving the two cops back from the cameraman, Murchison said, "Remember who helped you get the inside dirt on the Gacy killings when you were just a cub reporter covering community raffles?"

Keller was stone-faced. "Your call, Pat," she said softly.

Sighing, Murchison turned to Trebeck. "Let the son of a bitch go. This is the last thing the public needs to see. It's enough the bastards behind this have made us out to be idiots without showing how we're falling apart on this." He fixed his flinty gaze on Bolan. "However, was I you, Mr. Special Agent Fox, I'd damn sure keep my ass covered during the rest of this action."

Keller put the microphone back in her pocket. "One of these days you'll thank me for this."

"Not goddamn likely," Murchison growled.

"Can I quote you on that?"

The captain turned on his heel and began bellowing orders to his men.

Slinging his sniping rifle over his shoulder, Bolan wiped the blood from his lip. He spit, and it left a thick, dark web in the snow. Without another word, he turned and headed for the Blazer.

"Hey, wait up."

Bolan glanced over his shoulder and saw the reporter running after him.

"Goddammit, Fox, wait up."

Bolan kept walking.

"Look, I just saved your ass back there," she said as she drew even. "They wouldn't have hesitated at all about taking you apart. You owe me."

"What do you think I owe you?"

"The story. Your story."

"I don't think so."

Keller ran in front of Bolan, turned, placed a hand on his chest and blocked his way. "Do you have the idea that you're some kind of private army?" Her eyes searched his. "You're here chasing after some kind of demented military contingent, and you've alienated the Chicago police force in only hours. Don't you think you could use a friend?"

"No."

She shook her head. "You try to come across even harder than Murchison."

"There may be a reason for that." Bolan stepped around her.

"I want to make a deal with you."

"I'm not interested in deals." The warrior opened the door of the Blazer.

Keller put a hand on his arm. "I know where one of the hostages is being held."

Bolan looked at the reporter, then at the cameraman fifty yards away struggling to catch up. Ambulances had arrived at the stadium now, followed by fire trucks and cars containing television and newspaper people. He looked back at Keller and nodded. "Get in."

She smiled at her victory and turned to the cameraman, fishing briefly in her pocket. "Eric." The cameraman looked up. "Here's the keys to the car. Tell Rosewood I'll be in touch." There was a bright flicker that landed somewhere in front of the guy and was swallowed up by the snow. He dropped to his knees, cursing.

Bolan started the Blazer as Keller got in and slammed the door, then released the clutch and pulled onto the street. "If this doesn't turn out," he said, "I'm putting you out wherever we happen to be and you're on your own."

"Then maybe we should have taken my car." She was grinning when she spoke.

6

"It's a goddamned zoo out there," Quartermain complained. He stared out the second-story office window that overlooked South State Street, his arms folded across his chest.

Brognola silently agreed, but was sure he detected a note of wistfulness behind the man's words. Cars and news vans were scattered on both sides of the street, plumes of exhaust drifting from tail pipes as the people inside waited patiently. Occasionally one or more of the reporters would get out, stand in front of headquarters, do a bit in front of a camera, then climb hurriedly back into their vehicles. The big Fed took a fresh cigar from his pocket, unwrapped it, tucked it in the corner of his mouth, then dropped the cellophane into the wastebasket beside the desk. He checked his watch again, finding only five minutes had passed since the last time he'd looked.

Quartermain closed the blinds with a sigh as he turned to face Brognola. "There are a lot of people out there waiting for a statement to be released by the police department."

"It would get worse if you got up in front of those television cameras to tell them how little you knew."

"I suppose you're right."

"I know I'm right. Ignorance isn't supposed to be a political function." Brognola blinked his eyes, which felt heavy-lidded and scratchy.

Quartermain's smile was dry. "Touché," he said quietly. "But still, that's a city out there living in fear, and the people want answers from someone."

"They also want someone to be responsible for what's happening to them. Do you want to assume that role?"

"No."

"Then take my advice—let it ride."

"Even after the radio announcement?"

"Especially after the radio announcement." Brognola took the cigar out of his mouth. "Look, your people and mine are tracking that signal now. If there's anything to be found at Soldier Field, they'll find it." He glanced at his watch, irritated with himself when he realized what he was doing.

"We could use some good news. The department's still being raked over the coals for the fiasco your boy created at the bridge earlier."

The big Fed ignored the statement, more concerned with other matters. Knocking on the closed door to the hallway drew his attention.

"Enter," Quartermain said as he assumed the chair behind the desk.

The uniformed officer at the door looked haggard, her pale face washed out even further by the inferior lighting in the office. "Sergeant MacKensey told me to find you," she said. "Our units arrived at Soldier Field ten minutes ago."

"Why wasn't I told then?" Quartermain stood up.

Brognola glanced at the telephone on the desk. He'd given Bolan this number to call since it had an independent line and wasn't being used. That there hadn't been a call spoke volumes. His jaws tightened on the cigar as the familiar acidic pain in his stomach flared to new life.

"Things happened too quickly," the policewoman replied. "Three hostages are dead, and maybe as many as a dozen officers."

"Who were the hostages?" Quartermain asked on his way out the door.

Close on the heels of the policewoman, Brognola saw a grimace of distaste twist her tired features. Her eyes stared holes in Quartermain's back, and the Fed sympathized with her. Both of them knew Quartermain's interest was more political than personal.

The policewoman held on to her gun as she trotted to keep up with Quartermain's long strides. Brognola did the same, noticing how the activity in the halls picked up as soon as they hit the first floor.

"Two of them have been identified," the policewoman said as they caught the stairs for the communications room. "Winona Vandiver and Philip Coltrane. The remaining hostage was another woman, but she had no—"

"Philip Coltrane," Quartermain echoed as they entered the communications room. People were hurriedly logging information as it came in, monitoring the bursts of static that broadcast from the scene.

Brognola tried to track fleeting bits of the conversations, but the unconnected facts gave a disorganized picture. A chill raced up his spine as the litany of dead came through.

"Isn't he Mindy Coltrane's son?" Quartermain asked as uniformed police officers moved around them.

"Her youngest," the policewoman answered.

"Damn."

Brognola remembered the Coltrane name from the brief he'd helped put together for Bolan. There was money associated with it, as well as a covert political power in the city. The lemony look on Quartermain's face revealed thoughts of his political aspirations slipping away as surely as fog before a clear dawn. The big Fed didn't bother trying to feel sympathy for the guy. They moved in the same kinds of circles, maybe, but for a lot of different reasons.

Quartermain commandeered one of the dispatch officers and Brognola closed in on them, getting a thumbnail sketch on the trap at the stadium.

"Where's Fox?" Brognola asked when Quartermain had exhausted his small store of questions concerning Philip Coltrane and establishing the fact that Mindy Coltrane hadn't been notified yet.

"They don't know," the dispatch officer told him. "Agent Fox disappeared right after the attackers got away."

"Has the media arrived there?" Quartermain asked.

"Yes, sir."

"Make sure they're kept at a distance," Quartermain ordered, "and under no circumstances are the names of the deceased to be turned over to them. Understood?"

"Yes, sir."

After the dispatch officer relayed the message, Brognola asked, "Were any of the attackers taken into custody?"

"Not to my understanding."

"Were any taken dead?"

"According to the reports I've received, FBI Agent Fox accounted for some of the terrorists before he left the scene, but the bodies were recovered before the escape was made."

Brognola exhaled angrily. A solid lead on the people behind the terrorist activity remained as insubstantial as Quartermain's political ambitions were becoming.

"They're still searching through the remains of the announcer's booth," the dispatch officer said, "so there's still a chance something will turn up."

"The remains of the announcer's booth," Quartermain echoed.

The dispatch officer nodded. "Yes, sir. That's where the transmitting signal was issued. Agent Fox grenaded it while he was apparently pinned down under terrorist fire."

Quartermain fixed Brognola with a black look. "Grenaded it," he repeated.

"Yes, sir."

The big Fed dropped the remains of his cigar into an ashtray.

"What else did Agent Fox manage to do before he decided to leave?" Quartermain asked in a tight voice.

"Sergeant Trebeck says Fox was responsible for firing the first shot." The dispatch officer evaded Brognola's intent gaze.

Quartermain reacted instantly. "Instruct the men at the site that Agent Fox is to be taken into custody the next time they see him. Then notify everyone of lieutenant grade and above that there'll be a meeting in my office within the hour. They're to be on time."

"Yes, sir."

Turning to Brognola, Quartermain said, "Is there something you'd like to say?"

Brognola matched the man's gaze with an inner fire of his own. "You're chasing the wrong man. You should be concentrating on getting the people behind this thing, not splitting up your forces."

"Bullshit. You come down here throwing your weight around, bullying me and this department, and expect us to be grateful for your intervention. I don't give one good damn what you think of Fox or his methods. That man is at least as big of a menace to this city as the people he's supposed to be chasing. He's off the streets—as of this moment. You call him, tell him how it is, and maybe he won't get hurt, because, believe me, if it comes down to that, I won't hesitate."

Before Brognola could respond, an explosion slammed into the building, rocking it, filling it first with sound, then flickerings of lights that turned to black. The second explosion detonated a second after the emergency lights came on.

"WHERE'S THE HOSTAGE you mentioned?" Bolan asked Keller.

"I don't know."

The Executioner pulled the 4X4 to a stop at the side of the street, reached across the reporter and popped open the door. "Out," he growled.

Bolan rested his arms on the steering wheel as he surveyed the scattered traffic traveling both ways. A yellow dump truck scattering sand roared by them, moving painfully slow as the whump-whump-whump of the tailgate trailed in its wake. There was a lot of anger trapped inside the warrior, and he could feel it twitching restlessly, knowing the woman was unaware she was setting herself up to take the brunt of a major portion of it. "I don't have time for games, lady. I thought I made that clear."

"You did. You have." Keller pulled her parka hood back up, her eyes blinking furiously as snowflakes jetted into the Blazer. "Look, this is no gag. I'm taking you to someone who can tell us where a hostage is. Remember Vanessa Ellison?"

"The woman kidnapped off her father's yacht this evening?"

"Yeah. Well, I dug up a picture of her in the news morgue and had some copies ran off of a still of her taken at a benefit her father sponsored a few months ago. The police department was mobilized to find out how many possible hostages there might be and who they were. They don't have time right now to search for her, nor do they really have the clearance to say what this is all about. The way I figured it, while they were occupied with discovering how many people, as well as who, might have been kidnapped, I'd start my own investigation with the one person I knew for sure had been taken hostage."

Bolan stared into the dark eyes, seeking to read the mind behind them, relying on the instincts he'd honed over the years of unending war to guide him. Everything in him said she was telling the truth.

"Can I shut this door?" Keller asked. "I'm freezing my ass off here."

Bolan nodded.

Keller slammed the door, and the heater began its struggle to rewarm the interior.

"It was a long shot."

"Yeah, well, they pay off sometimes, too." Keller looked at him. "I'm coming to you with this for two reasons. One, because I want the story I know you represent. And two, because I've seen how the police department is set up to react to this situation. I'm thinking you're Vanessa Ellison's best chance of coming out of this thing alive."

"You're in the minority on that point."

She smiled. "Long shots and underdogs," she replied. "My old man was a gambler from the old school and believed in them both."

"Hell of a way to live your life."

She shrugged. "It gave him a way to view and understand his world, and maybe it helped me become what I am now."

"And what's that?"

"A woman who trusts her instincts."

"Maybe we have something in common," Bolan said as he eased the stick back into first gear. A faint smile touched his lips, dissipating some of his anger as he admired the reporter's gutsy attitude.

"I think we do," Keller said. "Otherwise I wouldn't have kept after you when you gave me the brush-off at the police department. The thing about gambling with money is that you can still get up from the table and walk away a loser. It doesn't work that way in your business."

Bolan didn't have an argument to her insight and remained silent as he edged back onto the traveled area on his side of the street. "What do you have on Vanessa Ellison?"

"Right before the fireworks at Soldier Field started, I got a call from a guy who said he knew where she was being held."

"Why didn't he tell you where she is?"

"I haven't paid him yet. And that brings me to another point. Do you have any money?"

Bolan looked at her in disbelief.

She opened her purse and took out some crumpled bills. "I've got sixty-three dollars."

"How much do you need?"

"A thousand."

"Are you sure this guy's good for the intel?"

"Isn't 'intel' a military term?"

Ignoring the question, Bolan said, "How do you know you're not going to get ripped off?"

"You're going to be there," she replied with a smile. "Besides, Jackie's been good for tips before. However, it gets more expensive the more he knows. That's why I think he's really on to something here. Otherwise he'd never have asked for that much."

"What makes you think he isn't going to sell it to someone else, or that he hasn't already?"

"You'll ask him not to. I think Jackie could really get into advice from you if it's presented well. And no one else I know would trust their editors or news directors to put up the cash."

"Where do we find him?"

"At Billy Goat Tavern. It's at 430 North Michigan, next to the Trib Building. It's a hangout for newspaper employees. My dad used to go there a lot when I was a girl. He wrote a lot of sports columns on that bar when he worked for the Trib."

"If this does pan out," Bolan said, "we're going to do this my way, which means you're nowhere near the action."

Keller hesitated. "All right, but I want to go on record as saying you're a damned thankless kind of guy."

"Maybe it's that sort of business."

KARL MOLTKE AIMED the rocket launcher at the police cruiser screaming toward his group's van. "Clear!" he yelled to his loader. The man clapped him on his free shoulder. Centering on the cruiser's grille, he squeezed the trigger and felt the immediate thrust of the rocket leaving the launcher.

The 94 mm warhead zipped over the snow with a rooster tail of sparks trailing it. The resulting explosion ripped the police cruiser from the ground for an instant as burned metal peeled back in ragged strips. An orange fireball engulfed the grille, highlighting the frantic efforts of the two patrolmen to escape just before the gas tank ruptured.

"Load!" Moltke called. The loader slammed a fresh warhead into the launcher and clapped him on the shoulder. Keeping the weapon in position, the metal bull's-eye target grid never far from his eye, Moltke surveyed the carnage his team had created.

Less than thirty seconds had gone by since the initial attack on the building. Brick and mortar littered the front of the building, and gray smoke curled outward from the deep pockets carved out by the warheads. At least a dozen bodies lay sprawled in the snow, black on white in the dark of night. Sporadic small-arms fire was being returned from the windows, but largely having no effect on the body armor the team wore. The news reporters who'd been waiting for a statement from the police officials had abandoned their vehicles and were engaged in filming the attack.

Moltke lifted his walkie-talkie as he surveyed a news van pulling from its position at the side of the street with a cameraman filming on top. "Erhard?"

"*Ja?*"

"In English."

"Yes, sir."

"Are you getting this on film?"

"Yes."

"Keep filming until I call the retreat, then make sure you get shots of what happens to the men attempting to follow us."

"Yes, sir."

Moltke pocketed the walkie-talkie, then aimed the launcher at the approaching news van. He could make out the driver enough to see the man wasn't paying attention to how close he was coming to the black-garbed warriors moving within the shadows of the street. He stroked the trigger, directing the warhead's flight toward the front tire on the passenger side.

There was no sense in killing the fools outright, and the cameraman might have footage at least as good as what they were supposed to get.

The rocket blew the wheel away when it detonated, rupturing the wheel well and tearing away a large section of the street. The van rocked uncertainly, then turned over on the driver's side with a tortured scream of metal. It continued skidding over the ice until it crashed into a parked car. The cameraman was thrown clear of the wreck, still holding on to his camera.

Moltke hoped it didn't break. He passed the launcher to his subordinate as he reached for the Heckler & Koch MP-5 SD-3 submachine gun suspended at his waist. He triggered short bursts toward the entrance of the police department, adding to the fusillade that finished splintering the glass from the doors and kept the officers inside pinned down. He didn't need to glance at his watch to know the numbers on the one-minute strike time had run down. He'd been counting since he'd fired the opening round. "Fall back," he said into the walkie-talkie.

The team moved back at once, clambering into the strike vehicles without question or hesitation, their retreat covered by .50-caliber machine guns mounted inside the Volkswagen vans.

"The steps," Moltke said to his immediate subordinate.

The man nodded, shouldered the rocket launcher, stepped forward to aim, then fired. The warhead streaked across the intervening space and struck the concrete steps, reducing a large portion of it to concrete dust and fragments.

Moltke climbed into the command car, a 240SL Mercedes as black as the vans, and watched the four vehicles move out ahead of him. He searched for Erhard and found the man still filming through the open doors of the last van.

The subordinate tossed the launcher in the back seat and followed it as Moltke gave the driver orders to proceed. He reached into the glove compartment as the Mercedes fishtailed across the street, removing a small electronic box. Something thumped into the front of the car. Moltke looked up in time to see a man's body roll up the windshield, then spill over the other side of the car.

"The fool ran out in front of me," the driver complained.

"No matter," Moltke replied. He returned his gaze to the back window as three police cruisers spun after them, throwing clumps of dirty snow behind them. He keyed the box to life as he extended the antenna. "Slower," he cautioned the driver. "Let them think they have us."

The man took pressure off the accelerator as the first bullets overtook them, smashing through the back glass. Bulletproof armor or glass had never been an option on any of the vehicles Dreyse had ordered. Speed was something they had all been trained to use, and the heavy weight of the armor would have been detrimental on the snow.

More bullets splatted against the Mercedes, at least two shredding foam and padding from the seats.

Hunching lower behind his seat, Moltke caught a flash of the fluorescent paint on the first of the light poles. He waited until he saw the third, then pressed the button on the remote control. Small explosions at the base of light poles, telephone poles and power poles toppled them into the street like so many matchsticks, creating a deadly blockage.

The first police cruiser tried to avoid the power lines that were suddenly sparking in front of it, only to skid wildly out of control on the snow. The power lines fell across the car and created artificial lightning bolts.

Moltke could almost smell the burned hair and flesh as he watched sparks jump through the police officers' hair. The thought made his skin crawl. The other police vehicles smashed into the first and became tangled up in the fallen lines, making passage by any following cars impossible. By the time pursuers made detours around the blockage, Moltke knew his team would be safely away.

Lifting the mobile phone, Moltke dialed the number of the van containing Erhard. "Did you get the film?"

"Yes, sir. I'm already duplicating it."

"Alert me the moment you've finished. We still have deliveries to make." Moltke hung up and settled back into his bullet-torn seat. He looked through the window at the city, amazed again at how ripe it was for the picking. It was as Dreyse had said—the Americans were totally unprepared for terrorist activity of this magnitude to take place on their soil. The only problem was the unidentified American who moved and fought so quickly. Moltke made himself relax by reminding himself that one man couldn't stand in their way for long.

BILLY GOAT TAVERN was in full swing when Bolan and Keller arrived. The news reporter led the way through the press of human flesh toward standing room only at the counter, casually returning familiar greetings from the other patrons.

Dressed in a trench coat to cover his hardware, Bolan knew he drew more than his share of attention. The bullet-riddled Blazer parked outside would attract a lot of onlookers, too, once it was noticed.

"Excuse me, Pete," Keller said, leaning over the shoulder of a man to attract the attention of the cook at one end of the counter. She pushed the rack of potato chips to the side. "Hey, Vince."

The young cook turned from the grill, flicking ash from his cigarette as he took it from his mouth. He squinted against the smoke, put his spatula to one side and wiped his free hand across the stained white smock. "Hey, Delaney, what can I do for you?"

"I'm looking for Jackie."

The cook gave her a white-toothed grin. "Hey, babe, you should upscale your goals. Instead of lookin' for hamburger, you should move on up to prime rib."

"Jackie?" Keller reminded.

"Somewhere in the back. Probably tryin' to get up a game of three-card monte with some of these stiffs."

"Thanks, Vince." Keller pushed away from the counter.

She made her way to the back of the tavern with difficulty, partly caused by the large number of people gathered there and partly because most of the other reporters kept trying to pump her for information. From the questions asked, Bolan gathered that most of these people were newspaper reporters waiting to turn into words the pictures the television people put together. Most of them seemed surprised and curious that she was off the street.

"Usually the only time you see this many people in here is at noon," Keller said to Bolan as she elbowed her way past a small group in the center of the floor.

Bolan identified Jackie Ching from the description Keller had provided on the way over. The man was tall and slim, with a shock of black hair cut in punk fashion. A dangling earring in his left ear glinted in the dim light, and he was dressed in black chinos and a lavender sweatshirt.

Keller caught the man's eye and continued walking toward the rest rooms in the back. When Ching passed through the men's room door, she didn't hesitate about going in after him. Aware of the attention drawn by their passage, Bolan followed.

The men's room was small, the usual porcelain accoutrements strategically placed to get the most from the limited space. Ching headed for a neutral corner, shoving his hands in his pockets as he placed his back against the wall. His eyes widened slightly when he saw Bolan.

"Aw, for Christ's sake, Delaney," a man standing at one of the urinals complained.

"Zip it up and put it away, R.J.," Keller said, "unless you figure it's worth feature space."

The man zipped with a black scowl, did a hurry-up job at the sink and left. Bolan took up position at the door, placing his foot so it effectively blocked entry. For the moment, the show was Keller's.

"What have you got for me, Jackie?"

Ching glanced at Bolan. "Who's he?"

"He's with me."

"You made the terms of the deal very specific, Delaney. You said just you and me, and the thousand bucks."

"He's the bank," Keller said. "I had to cut a new deal with him."

Ching rubbed the back of his neck. "If he's heat, then I'm in a lot of trouble for withholding information."

"You want trouble with the thousand or without it?" Keller flashed the money Bolan had given her.

Ching smiled. "That's a lot of money, but maybe it's not enough. You know what I mean?"

Keller kept her eyes on the man. "Meet Jackie Ching, the original almost-got-it-made guy. He does a small, occasional act at Zanie's while he waits to be discovered by the Second City people. Jackie's done about everything part-time, and maintains a lot of contacts for the occasional dip into drug connections, which is why I listen to him when he says he has some information."

Ching licked his lips carefully as his eyes switched from the reporter, to Bolan, then back again. "Look, there's no reason we can't keep this friendly."

"You're right," Bolan said in a graveyard voice. "The thousand's enough, and that's as friendly as it gets."

"Yeah, okay." Ching took the proffered money, counted it, then shoved it in a pocket.

"Where's the Ellison girl?" Keller asked.

Someone bumped against the men's room door. Bolan called out, "Busy," and didn't move. There was a muffled curse that faded away.

"Well, after you gave the picture to me, I started nosing around," Ching said. "Talked to a couple of buddies of mine, spread a little bread around of my own. That's why I was wanting to see if I could get more."

"The girl, Jackie," Keller prompted. "If I had all night to find her, I wouldn't be here making sure you got your money. I'd be out there looking myself."

Ching sobered up at once. "She's in Clancy's warehouse, down by the lake." He gave her the address. "I figure they took her there because the cops had already searched the area."

"This is probably the most important thing you've ever given me," Keller said.

"Yeah, well, you've been good to me over the years."

Keller stepped forward. "I'm not telling you that because I want you to know how much I appreciate it, Jackie. I'm telling you that because I want you to know how much grief you can bring on your own head by opening your mouth to anyone else about this. My friend considers this a wise investment for the moment. Let's do our bit to make sure it stays that way. Understand?"

Ching tried to smile, but it didn't work. "You won't have any problems from me." He stepped toward the door.

"Use the window," Bolan directed.

Ching looked at the window at the other end of the rest room. Snow covered most of the lower panes. "You're kidding, right?"

"No. Too many people saw us come in here with you. You need to vanish now, before you start getting too many tempting offers, or someone decides you know more than you need to and calls the police."

"I left my coat back there."

"Buy another. You've got a thousand dollars burning a hole in your pocket."

Ching looked like he wanted to protest further, but thought better of it. The window squeaked when he pried it open and let himself outside. Keller stepped through the snow that whirled in and closed the window.

She turned to Bolan. "Where do we go now?"

"After the girl."

"What about reinforcements?"

"This is a one-man operation. If it takes more, she wouldn't come out of there alive anyway."

"And you're willing to risk her life on your skills?" Keller's voice turned harsh.

"This isn't some kind of ego trip for me. This is what I do. So far the people responsible for the hostage situation have had the offensive. To be able to effectively strike back, we need some kind of leverage. Knowing who they are would be a nice start."

The reporter considered that in silence. "Where do I fit in?"

"If I don't make it, you get to call in the cavalry."

"There may be more hostages there than just the Ellison girl. If these people thought the warehouse was such a good idea, they may have brought more in."

Bolan nodded and opened the door, at once greeted by a press of people who suddenly tried to appear they were on their way somewhere else. He took the lead, the crowd moving away from him. Television programs were suddenly interrupted for special announcements. The reporters of the different channels started describing the daring raid on police headquarters that had so far resulted in fifteen dead and dozens injured.

The Executioner grabbed the woman's hand and pulled her after him, away from the pictures of violence cascading across the screens as silence gripped the tavern. Then they were merely the spearhead for the sudden exodus from the building as the newspaper reporters raced for their vehicles.

7

Bolan didn't risk a drive-by. With the snowstorm snarling traffic, such a maneuver would have been suspect to the hard team waiting inside the warehouse.

Delaney Keller remained silent as the warrior removed the trench coat and checked his hardware. The Desert Eagle and the Beretta rode leather in their customary positions. He slung the Franchi PA3/215 pump-action shotgun over his back in a customized shoulder rig. He left the sniper rifle with his other distance weapons, knowing this encounter would have to be close up and personal if it was going to be successful.

He smeared on combat cosmetics as Keller watched, aware that the reporter was curbing both her professional and personal curiosity as he prepared for war. Finished, he pulled on the watch cap, then donned two pairs of gloves, the inner pair of thin leather and the outer thick with insulation. He clipped a pair of tear gas canisters to his harness and reached for the door.

Keller's face was a tight mask when he looked at her, her dark eyes shiny with fear. "Stay inside," Bolan told her gently. "The key's in the ignition. Don't start the engine to keep warm because the exhaust from a sitting vehicle will draw attention either from the guys I'm looking for or from the police. Either event will send this whole operation down the tubes and endanger the people in there. The minute anything goes wrong, you slide behind this wheel and haul ass out of here. Wait until you're moving before you try calling that number I gave you. Understand?"

She nodded.

"Repeat it."

She did, her voice tight with tension.

"Keep your head down while I'm gone."

"How do you get used to this?"

Bolan gave her a small grin from the heart. "You don't. That's the last thing you want to do." He opened the door and stepped out.

"How will I know if something's gone wrong?"

"There'll be a lot of shooting," Bolan replied, "and I won't be back."

Her face showed that she wasn't sure how to take him. "Good luck."

He nodded and melted into the shadows.

Clancy's warehouse sat back from Lake Michigan in a neighborhood built up by the shipping business on the Great Lakes. From the scant intel Keller had been able to dig up through her station, the warehouse did booming business during the summer and was closed down much of the time in the harshest winter months. The alleys were narrow and winding, large enough to accommodate the diesel-powered forklifts that trundled loads to and from the docks, and narrow enough to provide a lot of cover.

The problem with cover was that it worked both ways. The Executioner found it difficult to see very far in any direction without taking the chance of being seen himself. Forced by the snow to remain on the ground rather than taking the high road along the rooftops, he hugged the sides of the buildings.

Halting in the alley west of the targeted warehouse, he crouched in the darkness and took the night glasses from a pocket. Clancy's was printed along a sign crowning the two-story structure sandwiched between two taller buildings. He tracked down, finding the rear door, visualizing the double doors that would face the lakefront. Windows were limited to two each on both sides that he could see, and all of them were on the second-story level well above his reach.

As he watched, a figure carrying an automatic rifle moved past the window on the south side, made lighter than the darkness by the infrared glasses. It instantly knocked the theory of a dry run. Knowing they had at least one guard circulating on the upper floor, Bolan surveyed the outside grounds for others.

Seeing nothing, he returned his field of view to the windows, timing the moves of the roving guard. There were two of them working equidistant from each other, taking twenty seconds to pass each window at a moderate pace. The creaking of the wooden sign along the top of the building sounded ominous, becoming louder then softer at odd moments as the wind rose and fell like waves from an atmospheric ocean.

The noise was an asset and he knew it. How to play off it was another matter. The people inside weren't just hostages in an elaborate kidnapping. They were prisoners of war in the minds of the men who guarded them. At the first show of force, they wouldn't hesitate to kill the hostages in instant retaliation.

Conscious of the time passing, Bolan waited until the windows were clear, then dashed across the open space to come up against the western side of the warehouse with the stubby SPAS PA3/215 clenched in his fist. He worked his way around to the side facing the lake, coming to complete halts when he knew the guards would be passing overhead.

The warrior tried to calculate how many guards might be inside, then gave up because he didn't have enough intel to go on. The number of guards would be in direct proportion to the number of hostages. Three men could have easily covered the Ellison girl. As an exercise in logic, it seemed like a waste of manpower. Then he reconsidered that fact. Not all of the hostages needed to be kept alive.

Waiting until the wind was rattling the tin overlaying the structure, he drove the tip of his combat knife through the metal, then stepped in front of it so that light wouldn't show through the new opening when he retracted the blade. He placed a lens of the night glasses over the triangular inch-long slash and studied the interior of the warehouse, careful to keep one hand shadowing the hole.

The orange glow of an electric heater in the southwest corner of the warehouse played over the four people huddled before it. Three of them, one woman and two men, wore pajamas. The other man wore street clothes. They all had on coats, hats and gloves.

Revealed in gray-black flashes, the rest of the warehouse looked empty, with only a few crates and pallets scattered across the concrete floor. There were four guards, counting the two keeping watch on the catwalk/storage space on the second floor. The other two remained at ground level well away from their hostages.

And there were skylights set on either side of the sloping roof.

Bolan used a fingertip of one of the insulated gloves to plug the hole as he moved away, and it flopped against the side of the building silently like a disembodied hand. He slid his other hand out of the remaining glove as he reached for the folding grappling hook and the thin nylon cord he carried in the blacksuit. The hook caught the brace holding the front of the big sign on top of the warehouse on the first cast.

The wind tore at him as he made his way up the side of the building. His mind clicked through the twenty seconds he had to work with as his arms pulled him upward. At seventeen he was straddling the rooftop and yanking the cord up after him.

Keeping a low profile to the wind, he tugged and skated his way to the southern skylight. After estimating the height of the warehouse at this point to be roughly twenty-five feet, he measured out ten feet of cord, then secured the measured length to the building rather than the sign again. Once he was in motion there was going to be two-hundred-plus pounds swinging from the other end.

He attached the free end of the ten-foot length to his ankle and tested the knots to make sure there wasn't enough slack in the noose to slip free, and that it wouldn't close up on him. Satisfied, he unleathered the SPAS PA3/215 and stepped toward the skylight, staying out of the field of view until the last minute.

Holding the slack in his free hand, he jumped through the skylight, shielding his face for a moment as glass rained down around him. He reminded himself the guards on the ground floor were his primary targets as the wrench of free-fall knotted his stomach.

The interior of the warehouse spun awkwardly as he resisted the impulse to right his descent. The cord would serve to keep him from landing on his feet anyway. Startled movement jerked below him, the hostages' faces becoming pale ovals as they looked up.

The Executioner hit the end of the cord with enough force to snap his teeth together and make him feel as if his spine had been driven through his skull. Then he was swinging with the arrested motion, the SPAS coming down in his hands almost too quickly as he sought target acquisition.

Bolan aimed for the first guard's exposed face, already discounting the chest area protected by the body armor. He squeezed as he twisted, pumping and following up the first shot immediately with a second before moving on to his next target. The double-aught buckshot ripped the flesh from the man's skull as the impact shoved him to the floor.

Autofire threw orange glare against the walls as the second-story guards searched for Bolan.

The soldier racked the slide and targeted his next man, arching his back against the swing of the cord to bring the guy into view. He triggered a round that took the guard chest-high, feeling the recoil after his swing. Pumping again, knowing there were no vulnerable areas available to him, he shot for the guard's rifle, blowing it out of the man's hands and sending him staggering and scurrying after it.

Dropping the useless shotgun, the Executioner ripped his combat knife free of its boot sheath, stroked it across the nylon, and fell the remaining distance to the concrete floor as the guard locked his fingers around the assault rifle and swung it toward the hostages.

"YOU LOOK LIKE you've been worked over by one of the pugs Manny Tusconi keeps on his payroll."

Trebeck finished pouring his cup of coffee from a thermos, then turned to face the speaker on his way back to his desk. "I guess you heard about it."

Captain of Detectives Mike Hanlon nodded. He was a big man, rough and craggy, with white shirtsleeves rolled up to mid-forearm, and a gauze patch taped above his right eye. "About you and the Feeb mixing it up? How was I supposed to miss that? I'm a detective, for Christ's sake." His tone sounded strained but not angry.

"How are things here?"

Hanlon sighed. "Total dead is up to twenty-one now, with four more not expected to make it to morning. Most of the power in the building has had to be rerouted to keep Quartermain's strategy session below going. That's why we're subsisting on emergency power and flashlights up here. Plus Brognola suggested it might be an idea to keep lights in the open areas to a minimum in case snipers are sent back later to keep us ducking. Of course, lights out won't be any defense against those damned Startron scopes, but it does help remind the guys working inside to keep away from the windows."

"Brognola? He's Fox's contact from Justice, right?"

"Yep. Head of the Feeb force. Good man from what I've heard, and quick when he's under the gun. Guy downstairs during the blast would have died if Brognola hadn't put a tourniquet on his leg. Still may have to amputate the foot, though."

"What about Quartermain?"

"You know what they say about kids and fools."

"Still up and around, huh?"

"And in the way."

"I heard he's pushing to pull the department back and to get a no-engagement policy going on until this thing is over."

"You heard right." Hanlon scratched his head. "Screw that, though. The uniforms are struggling to keep on top of the panic on the streets. Shootings are commonplace. People are killing each other out there thinking they're defending themselves. It's not a city anymore, it's a damn war zone."

"Fox isn't helping change that perspective in the slightest," Trebeck said in a controlled voice.

"Yeah, well, unofficially, we've been given orders to shut him down."

"How does Brognola feel about that?"

"Nobody's told him, but I think he knows just the same. Guy's cagey, been around a few corners of his own. You can smell cop all over him."

"I don't get the same scent from Fox," Trebeck said.

Hanlon nodded. "I heard about Jack and wanted to tell you I'm sorry. I know you guys went way back."

"All the way." Trebeck locked in the rage, channeling it so that it would work for him when the time came.

"I also know you're not in here to catch up on paperwork." Hanlon meaningfully tipped the flashlight on the corner of the desk with a meaty forefinger. "Feeb or not, this Fox guy isn't somebody you want to go after by yourself."

Trebeck didn't say anything.

"You listening to me, Joe?" Hanlon studied his face.

Trebeck leaned forward, making the swivel chair squeak, and counted points off on his fingers. "You're right about it being a battlefield out there, you know. I've seen the results of two of Fox's firefights. There isn't a whole lot to walk away from when he's finished. The attack on the police department was in direct retaliation to the shindig down at Soldier Field. You got two groups out there racking up points in body counts—one of them we still haven't identified, the other is Fox. Both of them come from military backgrounds, and neither of them give a shit about the civilian casualties as long as they get to play. Right now Fox is the only lead I've got to work with. I figure that if I find him, I'm at least close to the other people we're looking for. This is my city. Jack was my friend. I don't intend to see either of them go down without doing something about it. I want to know what Fox knows, because I think he knows more than he's letting on."

Hanlon stood up. "Officially I have to tell you to back off and don't risk making things worse while we try to contain the situation. Unofficially you give me a call the instant you get anything I can use." He rapped his knuckles on the wooden desktop and walked toward the door.

"And, Joe?"

"Yeah?"

"The attack on the department building wasn't a retaliatory effort. The bomb squad figures the plastic explosives used on the light and power poles took more than an hour to set up. That hit was planned before these wise guys blew into town."

Trebeck considered that as Hanlon disappeared. He picked up the flashlight, flicked it on, and started reading the years-old files he'd pulled from Records. He turned another page, finding black-and-white stills of the multiple homicides committed at a supper club called Giovanni's. He and Jack had been rookie patrolmen then and had been on the late-night shift when the squeal came in concerning the battle taking place at Giovanni's. The blood and wreckage had finally faded into memory over the years, but the action at the stadium had brought it all rushing back.

The file contained everything—evidence of police corruption engineered through Jake Vecci, the violent deaths of Arturo Giovanni, Larry Turk, Pete Lavallo and others who had a lock on organized crime in Chicago back during those days. Technical details of the strike against the Mob were in the fat bundle of papers. Above it all was the name of a man who'd come and gone through the wipeout before the ashes grew cold.

Trebeck tapped his finger on Mack Bolan's name.

TEN MINUTES after she was left alone in the Blazer, Delaney Keller took the keys from the ignition, pocketed them, pulled her coat tighter and stepped out into the whirling snow.

Fox would be as pissed as hell, but a story was a story—unless it was an exclusive. And she intended to make this one hers.

She followed the trail he'd left in passing, the snow already filling in the footprints. Brushing hair out of her eyes, she crowded in close to the buildings, wondering if she would even know what to look for and if this was really such a good idea after all. Images of the massacre at Soldier Field kept swirling in her mind. She forced herself not to cringe, remembering Fox's statement that a person never got used to his line of work.

Forcibly restraining her imagination, she came to a halt in the alley overlooking Clancy's. She fumbled in her pockets for the microcassette recorder and a compact 35 mm camera.

She eased the tension out of her voice, then spoke into the recorder. "This is Delaney Keller, Chicago Nine News, reporting live from a warehouse on Lake Shore Drive where an FBI agent has just gone in alone to attempt the rescue of some of the hostages, including Vanessa Ellison, daughter of Carter Ellison." She shut it off, then focused the camera, adjusting the shutter speed and hoping for the best.

Her breath wheezed in and out of her lungs as she made the short run to the warehouse. She was sure her heart stopped when the sharp sounds of gunfire shattered the stillness of the night.

Glass fragmented above Keller as a body spilled through the window. She shielded her face with her hands as she crouched for protection. The body plummeted to the ground and sank into the snowdrift between the buildings. The assault rifle the man had carried made a separate miniature crevasse just out of reach.

Keller had the camera to her eye and was taking pictures before she realized she'd taken it from her pocket. Three shots, then she was talking into the recorder again as she edged toward the rifle in the snow. "A man has just been shot and knocked through the second-story window above me." She hoped it wasn't Fox and had to steel herself not to run. Curiosity gave her the nerve to investigate. "Gunfire is still going off behind me, inside the building. At this point I don't know how many of the terrorists or hostages there are, but evidently the federal agent inside is still putting up a fight."

The man was dressed in black, lying on his back, clothing torn in two places over his chest to expose ceramic material that Keller recognized as bulletproof armor from a story she'd done on the SWAT team a few months ago. The mask he'd been wearing was twisted, the straps holding it askew on top of his head. Dark trails of blood streamed down the pale face from his nose and mouth.

Trading the recorder for the camera, she shot pictures of the man, barely aware that the warehouse was now silent. She took a total body shot, triggered the automatic focusing ability of the camera and moved in for the close-up.

Her finger froze on the button as another man appeared suddenly, reaching for her as frame after frame stuttered through the camera. One hand gripped the camera, the other sliding around her neck and shutting off her breath.

BOLAN HIT THE FLOOR and rolled, the combat knife up and ready. The remaining guard on the first floor brought around the M-16 in a short arc.

The Executioner launched himself at the man as autofire from above chipped a ragged line less than a yard away. He collided with the guard, hurling both of them from their feet as the assault rifle went off in his ear and hot brass singed his cheek. The guard's breath whooshed out as Bolan landed on top of him and struggled for control.

The screams of the hostages as they scrambled out of the immediate area were punctuated by the shouted commands from the two guards above.

Unable to use his rifle, the terrorist struck out with an elbow, smashing it into Bolan's forehead.

Ignoring the pain, the Executioner batted the arm away, then drove the sharp point of the combat knife into his opponent's neck, feeling it score against the spine and lodge there. He released the handle as the spray of hot blood covered his gloved hand, then rolled over. Bullets from one of the gunners on the second floor drilled through the dying guard, searching for Bolan.

Bolan unleathered the Desert Eagle and fired at the first guard he saw, while still making three-point contact with the concrete floor. He shot three rounds at the guard's chest as he struggled to his feet, knowing he'd missed at least once. The 240-grain rounds punched the man through the window behind him in a sprawl of arms and legs.

Two 5.56 mm tumblers from the remaining gunner's weapon smashed into the Kevlar armor Bolan wore and sprawled him backward. He slipped in a pool of blood and went down on one knee. He steadied the .44 in both hands, then drove his attacker to cover.

"Stay down!" he ordered the hostages as he picked up the nearest M-16 and glanced at the full magazine. He got to his feet and sprinted to the opposite wall, listening for the movements of the terrorist on the floor above him. He raised the assault rifle when he located the man and triggered 3-round bursts in quick succession.

The groan of pain let him know he'd scored on the guard's unprotected feet and legs. A moment later the man tumbled over the edge and smashed into the concrete floor. The unnatural angle of his neck left no hope for taking him alive.

Uncertain of the fate of the man he'd knocked through the window, Bolan crossed the warehouse to the hostages. "Everybody on your feet. I'm taking you out of here."

"Who are you?"

"FBI. Move it." Bolan rammed a fresh clip into the Desert Eagle and holstered it, removing two extra clips for the M-16 he cradled in one arm. He took the lead, heading for the rear door in case the hostage team had some sort of backup waiting out on Lake Michigan. A short burst from the assault rifle chewed through the lock, and the door swung open easily.

"No!"

Bolan recognized Keller's voice just before autofire drummed into the warehouse wall beside him. He moved in front of the unarmed people as he shouldered his M-16. The body armor he wore would provide some protection.

The reporter stood before him, held captive by the man behind her. She struggled in the guy's grip and kept him from lining up his weapon on Bolan or the hostages. The guy tightened his forearm against Keller's neck, bloody spittle leaking down his chin, and pulled her up roughly.

The Executioner's burst took the terrorist in the forehead and ripped him away from Keller. Bolan turned back to the freed hostages. "Get out of here. Find a phone and call the police department. They'll send someone for you."

The hostages edged away, trading looks between Bolan and the dead man. Once out of the immediate area, they ran.

Keller was on her knees, a camera working reflexively as she coughed, gagged and sucked air back into her lungs. "Dammit," she complained hoarsely as she forced herself to her feet, "that was my story you just let get away."

"You're free to follow them."

"You son of a bitch!" she exploded as she followed him, glancing over her shoulder wistfully at the alley where the hostages had disappeared. "You just shot that man while he was holding me. Aren't you even going to ask me how I am?"

"You're sounding better all the time," Bolan commented dryly. He stepped his pace up to a trot. The Chicago troops would react within minutes.

"Hey, wait up."

Bolan slowed down a little, conscious of the fact that more of the terrorists might be within the vicinity, and the woman, for the moment, was still his responsibility.

"Where are we going?" Keller asked.

"I've still got a job to do." Bolan swung open the door of the Blazer and climbed inside. He reached for the ignition, then turned to the reporter and held out his hand. "Give me the keys."

Keller stepped back. "I want to make a deal."

"The deals are over."

"Not while I have the keys."

"Your choice, Keller. You can take this story and run with it, or I can place you under arrest for obstructing a federal agent in the course of his duty, and you can sit it out for a while. By the time you get loose, your story will be part of history."

"You're bluffing."

Bolan reached into the glove compartment and took out a pair of handcuffs. "Lady, I don't have time for bluffing."

She threw him the keys, then ran around the 4X4 and got in.

The warrior let out the clutch as the big tires dug into the snowdrifts between the alleys, heading for the warehouse. He pulled to a stop at the rear door, got out, and left the engine idling.

Keller dug out her camera.

"Put that back in your pocket," Bolan growled as he grabbed the lapels of the first dead man and tugged the body to the back of the Blazer, "or I'll confiscate it."

"Come on," the reporter said in exasperation. "The deal for the information I had was for your side of the story."

Bolan opened the back of the 4X4 and shoved the corpse inside. "The deal was for you to stay with the vehicle."

"I thought you might need help."

Bolan raised an eyebrow.

She shrugged. "I guess I underestimated you."

Still carrying the captured M-16, the warrior walked into the warehouse. He recovered the SPAS PA3/215 on his way out with the second body.

"Aren't you going to tell me about you?" Keller asked as she followed him back in. "About why you're here, acting more or less on your own?"

"No."

Her hoarse voice turned angry. "You fucking ingrate. You used me."

Bolan gave the woman a thin smile as he dragged the third body out by the heels. "Maybe we used each other a little, but I don't think either one of us is going to suffer a lot of guilt over it."

A ghost of a smile touched her lips.

By the time Bolan piled the fourth body on top of the collection he had in the rear of the Blazer, the compartment was full. He closed the hatch and locked it.

"Where to now?" Keller asked as she circled the 4X4.

The warrior reached across the passenger seat and locked the door before she could open it. He closed his door and locked it, as well.

"What the hell is this?" the woman yelled through the window.

Bolan thumbed the button to lower the window so he could be heard. "This is where the partnership ends. I'm headed for no-man's-land after this, and I don't need the extra baggage.''

"Extra baggage? You arrogant bastard, you can't leave me out here like this.''

"There's a heater inside the warehouse,'' Bolan replied as she shifted into reverse. "It'll keep you warm until the police arrive.'' He backed away and she ran after him for a moment, finally coming to a stop when she realized he really was leaving her.

"You better hope you never have to ask me for another goddamned thing!'' she yelled.

Bolan pointed the Blazer toward Lake Shore Drive, already hearing the scream of approaching sirens. "I do,'' he muttered as he watched the woman in the rearview mirror. Once on the street, he lifted the phone and dialed Brognola's number to arrange for the real VICAP team to be on hand at their meet.

8

"Would have been nice if you'd left us some faces to work with here," FBI Agent Frederick Haskell told Bolan as he circled the four bodies on the floor of the motel room, taking photographs.

The stripped corpses lay on overlapping plastic drop cloths while the VICAP team worked over and around them. The knife still protruded from the one man's throat and had caused Haskell even more problems with the photography.

Bolan stood in one corner of the room with Brognola, beside a coffee maker someone had plugged into an outlet. A sack of foam cups leaned against the wall and a blue can of coffee. Bleary-eyed, the warrior watched the information gathering with interest.

The motel room looked as if it had been ransacked by vandals. The bed had been overturned, upended and placed against the wall over the room's only window to block the view afforded by the threadbare curtains. The rest of the furniture had been stacked in the small closet and by the bed. The only thing that seemed organized was the tidy pile of manila file folders they continually added to. The television, tuned to the local channel Bolan knew Keller worked for, sat on the floor while its stand was being used as a makeshift desk.

"What the hell are you bitching about, Freddie?" another agent asked as he knelt beside one of the corpses and took fingerprints. "You got two perfectly good faces there to work with."

"Yeah, and one of them could be laid out in the front yard and used as a sundial with that knife sticking in him like that."

"Come on," a third agent said with a chuckle as he put the dead men's personal effects in separate plastic sandwich bags, "it's not like we're going to throw these guys back and hope for a better catch next time."

Haskell dropped the 35 mm for a Polaroid One-Step and started the lineup again. "Oh, yeah, I'm bitching. How many fingers you got to work with there? Five on a hand, right?"

Bolan checked the time and found it to be ten minutes after four. Another two hours and the city would be waking up to take on the new day. "How soon before we find out about these guys?" he asked.

Brognola took the cigar out of his mouth to reply. "Depends on their histories. Aaron's standing down now, waiting for us to come on-line and fax him everything we have. If they're clean, we're back at square one."

Bolan poured more coffee into his cup and walked closer to survey the dead men. "They've got a history somewhere, bet on it. See the scars? Knife, gun, the occasional burn, all of which they didn't get sitting back somewhere watching the world go by. I've got a feeling the assaults on the cities have been the quietest action they've seen for some time. Mention to Aaron that he might find some intel on them in the known merc units."

"I've already made a note."

The fourth FBI man emerged from the bathroom and jerked a thumb over his shoulder. "Darkroom's prepped when you get set for it, Freddie."

The man with the camera nodded. "I was waiting on you." He picked up the 35 mm camera and the two rolls of film he'd shot earlier, grinning as he walked by Bolan. "Who knows, Fox? Maybe I can cut a deal with *Fangoria* magazine for some of the stills. Special effects ain't got nothing on the job you do."

"You got a couple of shooters here," the fingerprint man said. He held up a hand, indicating the dark flecks trapped in the skin between thumb and forefinger. "Notice the permanent tattooing from powder burns?"

Bolan nodded.

"These guys have seen a lot of action to have acquired that much tattooing."

"Or they've had a lot of practice on the marksman range and in drills." Bolan crossed the room to the lawn and leaf bags that held the clothing taken from the corpses and took out pieces of the black uniforms. "These guys weren't just mercs, they were military at one time."

"What makes you say that?"

The warrior indicated a button on an overshirt stained with dried blood. "This was hand-sewn, not machined on. See how it was threaded through only two of the buttonholes instead of through all four?"

"Yeah, I can remember doing some of that myself back in Korea during parade dress." The big Fed flicked the button with a thick forefinger.

"It also tells us the guy ramrodding this operation is military when he's working. Details mean a lot to him."

"Also helps keep the troops in line," Brognola observed, "because it's the same kind of life-style they're accustomed to."

The fingerprint man slid a thumb into one of the corpses' mouths and pried it open. "I think you're dealing with guys who have a European background."

"Why?" Bolan asked.

The agent displayed the open mouth. "This guy had some real serious dental problems." Light gleamed from metal fillings and bridgework laced through the teeth. "He had some good work done to take care of it, which could fit your theory of a military past of some sort since they take care of those things, but the tip-off is the material used. These fillings are gold. American dentists quit using it years ago when it got too expensive and good ceramics were introduced, but European dentists haven't. This guy's too young to have received treatment here in the States to get fillings like that."

Brognola stuck a finger in his collar to loosen it. "With the way the walls are tumbling down in the ComBloc countries and democracy is rearing its ugly head, a trail back in that direction could be one of the last things we need. It would be easy to unsettle a lot of people who are already concerned over current events."

Bolan nodded and said, "We may not have a choice. You can't ignore it and hope it goes away."

Brognola looked glum.

"Have you found out anything about the payoff?" Bolan drained his coffee cup.

"No, so far everything's been quiet."

"Do you get the feeling someone knows something but isn't telling?"

"Oh, yeah, but that's a cheap feeling to come by. Justice is strictly persona non grata in Chicago at the moment. In fact, I wanted to talk to you about that."

The Executioner looked at his friend and said softly, "You're not going to ask me to back off now, are you?"

Brognola sighed. "Much as I'd like to, for your own sake, no. This is something that needs to be seen through to the end, and you're the best man for the job. Let's face facts here—every politician in this town is more concerned over his or her political salvation after this is over. If we can't put a stop to the person behind this, the same thing is going to happen again next month in some other city."

"If they stick to the schedule they've apparently set up for themselves."

The big Fed took out a fresh cigar and clamped it between his teeth. "They'll stick to it if they come out of this mess. Next time they'll just play things a little closer to the vest." He stared at Bolan. "And next time you may not be as accessible. If things go badly in this burg, the investigations into Justice's performance will be unavoidable, and those people are going to want to know everything they can about one Special Agent Fox. Then we have to look at the possibility that the successes these people have had may inspire copycat operations in other metropolitan areas. That will divide whatever federal forces we're able to field. No, it's got to stop here."

Bolan silently agreed as he surveyed the dead men on the floor, thinking again how much easier things might have been if he could have taken one of them alive. But even then time would have been working against him. America had never known true terrorism on her shores, but she was definitely getting a taste of it now. Efforts to rescue American hostages in other countries had been hamstrung by public opinion. Given time, he was sure the same thing would occur in American streets as they were converted into battlefields. He looked at Brognola. "I don't suppose I need to ask about the chances of getting a helicopter through the Chicago Police Department?"

"No. If you show up anywhere around there, it's more than even money that they'll lock you up. Quartermain's already pushing to have you sidelined. We had to flush a couple of tails to make this meet."

"Don't they realize they have to take a stand out there?" Bolan asked.

The fingerprint man glanced up and gave the warrior a crooked grin. "You've got to remember this is America. If you throw enough money at your problems, you can buy your way out of everything. Have you taken a look at our legal system lately?"

Bolan crumpled the cup, dropped it in the plastic wastebasket, then ran a hand across his face, feeling the stubble along his jaw. His eyes burned and his lids felt heavy. He glanced at his watch again. It was almost four-thirty, and he was still miles behind his quarry.

"Hey," one of the agents called out, "take a look at the television."

Bolan did, catching a view of the first police helicopter exploding over Soldier Field.

Brognola reached down and turned up the volume.

"...to let you know what you are facing," a clipped male voice was saying. "As you can see, your police force is drastically outmatched, and to continue to challenge us in this manner is not only foolhardy, but deadly as well." On-screen, the second helicopter blew up, revealing the filtering effect of the camera.

"I didn't know the press got any footage of that," Brognola said.

"They didn't," Bolan told him. "The terrorists took this themselves from the announcer's booth."

The scene vanished, at once replaced by the three bodies suspended from the goalpost. A black-garbed man stepped into view of the camera and lighted up the faces of the dead, one by one, as the narrator announced their names.

"Jesus," the fingerprint man breathed.

Bolan moved closer, shutting out the chill that drew his attention to the bodies, and concentrated on the voice and the movements of the man.

"We didn't want to kill these people," the narrator said as the camera zoomed in for a close-up of each face, "but we found it necessary to convince you of our resolve. To continue to hunt us will only end in other tragic deaths that can be easily avoided by complying with our demands."

The scene faded away, replaced by a visibly shaken anchorman who shuffled papers in front of him. "The tape you have just seen was delivered to this station by people who claim to be part of the terrorist group holding the hostages. Following this is another tape, also filmed by the terrorists, of the attack earlier tonight on the Chicago Police Department." The anchor looked away, obviously checking the station's private screen.

A montage of shots sped by silently, showing the destruction left in the wake of the assault on the police headquarters. Uniformed officers lay spread-eagled in debris-covered snow. Flames lapped eagerly at the cavity where the front doors had been, throwing garish shadows over the twisted metal frames. A police cruiser exploded.

The tape ended abruptly as the cameraman was obviously whisked away.

Bolan replayed the scenes in his head, searching for a nagging detail that bothered him. "What were the assault teams driving?"

"Volkswagen vans," Brognola replied. "Pretty much like the one we encountered on the bridge."

"They used Volkswagen vans at the stadium strike, too."

"I don't understand the connection."

"Those vans are part of the equipment these guys were trained on," Bolan explained, reaching for his coat. "The West Germans use them for their GSG-9 counterterrorist groups, along with a lot of the hardware we've seen so far. When you talk to Aaron, have him concentrate on that and see what he can pry loose."

"Relations in that part of the world are pretty strained right now. With the Wall coming down, every country big enough to stick out a hand is trying to get a finger in the pie."

"Have him do the best he can."

"Where are you going to be?"

Bolan opened the door and gave his friend a grim smile. "I think I know where I can get a helicopter."

KONRAD DREYSE MIXED himself a drink at the small bar in the yacht's saloon while he watched the television. Moltke sat on the long couch, his assault rifle laid out beside him as he refilled magazines.

The television station was replaying the tapes he'd sent. Farther down the hallway leading to the bedroom, a guard stood in front of the door with an Uzi slung around his neck. There had been no recent outbursts from the mayor and his wife. The yacht rocked slowly with the motion of the lake, and the heater pumped thick air through it.

Moltke picked up the magazines, shoved them into the deep pockets of his black flak jacket and took the drink Dreyse offered him.

"You did good work at the police station," Dreyse commented as the footage rolled across the screen. "It's reported that over two dozen men died as a result of your actions." He seated himself in a plush chair. "Is there any word on the team that was holding the Ellison girl and the others?"

Moltke shook his head. "Not yet."

Dreyse controlled the anger that coursed through him. He sipped his vodka, remembering the days when he wouldn't touch alcohol during a mission. But then he'd been under orders not to. Now, his indulgence symbolized the luxury of command and made the taste all the sweeter. Something he'd grown accustomed to.

"Maybe we should rethink next month's operation," Moltke said hesitantly. He couldn't maintain eye contact and glanced back at his glass as he swirled its contents.

"Getting cold feet, Karl?" Dreyse asked in a lightly mocking tone. "Come now, you've seen what we can do. This is the land of the fatted calf, and now's the perfect time to make the most of it."

"Still, we don't know much of the man who has confronted us at so many turns."

"And you let the thought of one man give you pause?"

Moltke remained silent.

"That isn't like you."

Moltke's grip tightened on the glass, his knuckles whitening. Then they relaxed. "I've seen this man in action. He isn't to be dismissed lightly. In fact, I've been thinking he's responsible for the disappearance of the hostage team in the warehouse."

"Why?"

"Because it was the work of one man."

"How do you know that? No one else has mentioned this."

"Because I could feel it. You know what I'm talking about, Konrad. I've seen you walk into a battleground and know things without knowing quite how you knew them as well. It was one man. I know."

Dreyse frowned and downed another quarter of his drink, feeling it burn along the back of his throat. He didn't like the thought of his troops becoming spooked. He'd trained most of them himself in one theater or another, and trained them in obedience to him foremost. One man wasn't going to strip that away. "Perhaps it's time to make another demonstration to the people of Chicago," he said softly.

Moltke looked up. "In what way?"

Setting his drink to one side, Dreyse leaned forward and smiled. "By killing this federal agent. I want you to find him for me, Karl, and I want him killed. Then drag his body through the streets so all can see what happens to those who dare challenge us."

"We haven't been able to find him. It's as if he's as insubstantial as smoke. And the police have been searching for him as well. He's nowhere to be found."

"He can be found," Dreyse said. "We just haven't been looking in the right places yet. This man will be drawn to us again as surely as the moth is drawn to the flame."

"But it won't be only the moth in danger." Moltke's voice was quiet but firm.

"Those are fine, young German boys out there, Karl. They won't back away from this man."

"No. We've trained them too well for that."

"Exactly. Perhaps this man is as dangerous to us as you say. If so, that's all the more reason to take him down now, to ensure he can't follow us or survive to trouble us again."

Moltke didn't look comfortable with the thought.

The television drew Dreyse's attention. He reached for the remote control and turned up the volume as the scene shifted from the regular anchorman to a dark-haired woman.

"Thank you, David," the woman said. "The following photographs were taken an hour ago at a warehouse near Lake Shore Drive where I was party to a rescue attempt by a federal agent that resulted in the freeing of four of tonight's hostages."

"I know that woman," Moltke said. "She was also at the stadium tonight."

Dreyse waved him to silence.

The television screen blinked, replacing the woman with a still of the warehouse. "Earlier," the reporter said, "we saw tapes provided by the terrorists who have invaded our city that demonstrated their strengths. Tonight I was on hand to see how one agent is laying his life on the line to free us from this nightmare." The television blinked again, depicting a man dressed in black standing over a body.

"There were four terrorists in this warehouse," the reporter went on, "and there were four hostages waiting to be executed if that's what their captors decided to do. That all changed when FBI Agent Thomas Fox found out their location and took matters into his own hands." Shots of the freed hostages followed, showing them coming out of the warehouse and vanishing down the alley.

"You say this woman was also on hand for the trap at the football stadium?" Dreyse asked, unable to take his eyes from the television, unable to keep from wondering how one man had taken a warehouse held and defended by four of his shock troops without losing one of the hostages.

"Now at least four families no longer have to worry if members are being held hostages," the reporter said. "And I for one am not convinced the suggested hands-off policy of the law-enforcement people working this case is the way to go. The terrorists are still out there, waiting. Even if we make it through this night, what is there to ensure this nightmare won't reach out again next year, next month or even next week?'' The segment ended with a series of stills.

"She was there," Moltke said.

The anchorman, visibly disturbed by the broadcast, rustled his papers and tried to collect his thoughts. "That was Delaney Keller, reporter for this station, in a personal story of the tragedy facing all of Chicago. Now on to a recap of the attack on the police department as more names of the dead are released...."

"There's your answer, Karl," Dreyse said. "Evidently this man and woman are working together in some capacity to arouse aggressive feelings in the city populace and dissuade them from acting in their own best interests. Find the woman, and you'll find the man. Then kill him."

"THAT WAS a great bit, Delaney."

Keller looked up from the sofa in the television station's small lounge to see her cameraman standing over her. She smiled, amazed at how close she was to sleep when the story was still waiting out there to be had. "Thanks, Eric. Sorry about stranding you back at the police station."

The man grinned as he plunked change into the bright red soft drink machine. "At least I didn't have to walk as far as you did." A soda can thumped into the trough and he dragged it out. "Can I get you something?"

Keller rubbed her eyes with the heels of her palms. "A diet soda, please." When he handed it to her, she pressed the can to her forehead and hoped the sudden chill would further revive her.

"I hear the police who arrived at the scene after Captain Marvel dumped you weren't exactly friendly either." The cameraman took a seat in the chair opposite the sofa.

"Captain Marvel?" Keller echoed.

Eric grinned. "That's what Rosewood's calling him. Says what else can you call a guy who arrives on the scene when trouble is everywhere, then does his civic duty to put said trouble down, and rides off before anyone can get a fix on him. Personally I think Rosewood is waiting for the call from the person who's seen this guy changing into tights in a phone booth."

"This is Rosewood, our no-nonsense news director, saying this?"

"Pretty fucking incredible, isn't it?"

Keller popped the top on the can and took a sip.

"Rosewood also figures this guy could be a big draw for a news feature after the terrorists clear out of the city."

"He's that sure they're going to clear out?"

"Oh, yeah. Rosewood's buddies with Mitch Tabor, who told him the payoff's already been arranged. By nine o'clock tomorrow, this will all be history."

"*The* Mitch Tabor?"

"Very same."

"I didn't know Rosewood knew Tabor."

"Neither did I."

"How is the payoff going to go down?"

"He didn't say." The cameraman sipped his drink and waggled his foot. "However, he did hint several times that if you could get this guy into the station for an interview, it would probably be worth a bonus."

"I doubt I'll hear from him again. I forced my way onto him the first time by promising him the moon. We didn't exactly part company with promises to swap Christmas cards. And I don't think he's the type to go in for a lot of publicity."

A man with a blue-leaded pencil tucked behind one ear stuck his head into the lounge and looked at Keller. "There's a call for you on line three, Delaney."

"Who is it?"

"Some guy. He didn't leave his name."

Keller crossed the room to the phone mounted on the wall and punched three. "Keller." She recognized the voice at once, and a mixture of feelings cycled within her.

BOLAN SAT on the passenger side of the Channel Nine helicopter and used his night glasses to scan the Chicago streets. Snow patterns, altered by the beating rotors, continued to cascade against the Plexiglas bubble. The ride was rough, made worse by the pilot's need to dodge through skyscrapers as he stayed as close to ground level as was safe.

"I was telling somebody just before you called that we'd probably never see each other again," Keller said. She sat in the rear of the chopper with another pair of night glasses. "I told him I didn't have anything else to offer you that you might find interesting. I guess I forgot about the helicopter."

Bolan grinned despite the seriousness of the situation. The lady's gutsy and cheerful attitude was definitely as welcome as it was unexpected. "You didn't mention you had one earlier."

"I wouldn't have this one now if I hadn't told my news director I was getting an exclusive interview with you out of this."

The warrior looked back over his shoulder at her.

She ignored him. "Look, I know you can't promise anything, and even if you could, there'd be some areas we'd have to skip over. I can get enough of a story from this to handle anything my director wants to throw at me. It might not be the one he's expecting, but I'm betting it's enough to keep some bubblehead out of my co-anchor spot on midday news. I'm a gambler's kid, remember?"

Bolan chuckled. "What kind of odds are you giving yourself on keeping the job?"

"Seven-to-three against, but I like long shots."

"If somebody was making book on it," Bolan said as he turned back to the night glasses and refocused his burning eyes, "I'd put my money on you."

"Thanks, but it won't do any good to try to butter me up. I still think you need a swift kick in the crotch for dumping me out at the warehouse. Did you find anything on the bodies?"

"No."

"Then what are we doing up here looking for Volkswagen minibuses?"

"The tapes the terrorists gave the news stations tipped me to this. That, and remembering the ones I'd encountered earlier."

"They've got a thing for Volkswagen minibuses?" the woman asked. "Or do they own a dealership?"

The reporter's words chunked through Bolan's conscious mind and he filed them away. Out of the mouths of babes, he thought in grim humor, but he didn't reply.

"Hey, Dean, can't you get any more heat out of this crate?" Keller complained.

The pilot shook his head. "You're getting the best of it now. These bastards are just cold in this kind of weather. And I got a news flash for you guys—we're only staying up as long as I got deicer, then we turn around and fill up again."

Bolan listened to the police-band radio tucked under the chopper's console. The listings of accidental shootings and prowler reports continued to pour in, taking up precious man-hours.

"How's the payoff going to be made?" Keller asked.

"I didn't know there was going to be one for sure," the warrior replied.

"There is, but I haven't heard how. Hoped you could help me out with that. How were the payoffs made in Dallas and San Francisco?"

"Electronic transfer of funds," Bolan replied. "Once they were on their way, the hostages were released and the terrorists vanished."

"Couldn't someone have tagged the transfers?"

"Officially the banks didn't want to risk it. Unofficially there was a trace, but it petered out once it crossed over into Switzerland. These people haven't used the same account numbers so far."

"I thought Swiss banking was impregnable, at least that's why they told me the Mafia guys used to launder their money through them."

"With the drug business on the rise in their own country," Bolan said, "Swiss bankers and the government have broken down some of the privacy barriers."

"The CIA got tagged on a couple of accounts they had there, too," the pilot said with a short laugh. "I remember when that went down."

"So the monies were trailed to Switzerland, then what?" Keller asked.

"Then it disappeared."

"In other words, if we don't find a lead somewhere in this mess before the terrorists blow town, chances are they'll get away with it again."

"Maybe," Bolan replied. "This time we've got a few other irons in the fire, too."

"You weren't there at Dallas or San Francisco, were you?" Keller asked.

"No. Not until afterward."

"I didn't think so."

The interior of the helicopter grew quiet, filled with the tension of the rotors beating overhead. Bolan ignored the cold seeping in through the Plexiglas bubble, scanning every pair of headlights he found on the snow-covered streets. It was after five. Soon dawn would arrive, and there'd be no time left to attempt the discovery of the terrorists. It was maddening to think that they were down there—so near, yet so very far. He hoped Kurtzman could turn up something with the information the VICAP team was faxing, but he wasn't as cheery about long shots and underdogs as

Keller appeared to be. He wanted something definitely more tangible.

Red lights flashed in the periphery of the warrior's vision as the Channel Nine helicopter swung out over Lake Michigan to cover the shipping areas. Bolan tracked the motion, catching a glimpse of the unmarked big Bell helicopter as it passed.

"We've got company," the pilot said as he reached for his radio.

A ragged line of bullet holes stitched across the pilot's side of the copter. The man sighed and collapsed across the controls, dead eyes staring sightlessly as blood leaked into them from a head wound.

Bolan muscled the man's body from the yoke as more rounds chewed up the rear rotor and pierced a hydraulic line. Abandoning thoughts of attempting to fly the aircraft, the warrior unlocked his door as the attacking Bell swept back into view and sprayed more bullets into the cockpit.

Lake Michigan spun crazily below as the newscopter tilted and started to lose altitude. Bolan shrugged out of his harness, slipped his boot knife free, grabbed Keller by the belt before she could move and slit her harness. He kicked out with a foot as he pulled the woman toward the open door, then they were in the slipstream, falling toward black and freezing waters as the attacking helicopter banked toward them.

9

Holding Keller in tight, conscious of the proximity of the failing helicopter and the danger of the whirling blades, Bolan controlled their fall, getting their feet under them. The rushing air shredded the reporter's scream, which turned the warrior momentarily deaf as he searched for the attacking helicopter. Machine-gun bursts followed their descent, then the wine-dark waters embraced them, shutting out all light.

Keller struggled against him, silvery bubbles escaping from her lips. The water rushed up around them as they were drawn farther down. He couldn't release the woman and slow their descent for fear of losing her in the deep black.

The pressure on his ears was unrelenting, threatening him with unconsciousness. A yellow fireball ignited on the lake surface thirty feet or more above them, spitting a liquid inferno in all directions that burned briefly and disappeared. For a moment nothing surrounded them and they were trapped in zero gravity, then buoyancy tugged at them, directing them toward the surface.

Keller fought against him, tried to force his hand away from her mouth and nose, tried to bite him when that failed. The warrior kept kicking them steadily upward, not giving in to the raw pain burning in his own chest. When the woman stopped moving, he pulled her face level with his and looked into her eyes. A bright sheen of controlled fear shone back at him. He covered her lips with his and gently released half of the air he'd sucked into his lungs before the water took them. Her breath was hot and warm as her hands slid behind his neck and took the air greedily.

Breaking away gently, Bolan pulled them toward the surface. It seemed lighter above them now, but he still couldn't judge the distance. His heartbeat sounded slow, and black comets danced before his eyes, changing orbits whenever the mood struck them. He felt the cold now, biting into his flesh, and realized the woman had to be hurting more than he was. If the depths didn't get them, there was still the almost freezing temperatures of the lake that would surely drag them down again before they could make shore.

Bolan's hand slid out of the water only an instant before he got his head up. Keller was a limp weight at the end of his arm. He treaded water as he forced her up, tucking her head under his chin as he went over on his back. For a moment he thought he'd lost her, then he heard the first hacking sob that signaled an intake of breath.

Bits and pieces of the helicopter floated past as traces of the burning fuel reserves wheeled around them like floating candles. The pilot's corpse was nowhere to be found.

Rotors screamed overhead as a searchlight swept across them, paused, and arced back in their direction.

"Down," Bolan commanded, rolling over and shoving the woman under the water again. His hand felt like an arthritic claw as he drew the Beretta 93-R from soaked shoulder leather. He let the barrel drain, popping the magazine out to hurry things along, kicking the round in the pipe loose in the lake, then slammed the magazine back home and released the action to strip the first 9 mm hollowpoint into the chamber. He heard Keller surface again somewhere behind him as he slid down, leaving only his hands and his head from his nose up exposed.

He flicked the pistol to 3-round burst and attempted something of a T-stance in the lake as he targeted the Plexiglas bubble of the helicopter screaming along less than ten feet above the water. The Beretta's flash suppressor would keep their gunners honest, relying on the searchlight to find their quarry.

The Executioner curled a finger around the trigger as he unfolded the 93-R's short stock, then squeezed off the first two bursts. Spiderwebs broke across the bubble, causing the pilot to pull up sharply. The helicopter passed by less than a dozen feet overhead, trailing bullets as two shooters leaned out wide to track him.

Bolan spun in the water, lifting the Beretta in one hand as he focused on the guy clinging to the port side. Mentally he became the sniper scope he needed, then caressed the trigger. The gunner dropped like a rock and disappeared under the lake.

A Klaxon whined and drew the warrior's attention to the police boat speeding toward them.

"Start swimming toward the boat," Bolan commanded. The woman went into motion at once. He followed, stroking one-handed to keep the Beretta out of the water.

The helicopter heeled around and came back faster than before, closer to the lake's surface. Bolan waited, the wind from the whirling rotors pushing against him before he returned fire.

The remaining assault rifle spit 5.56 mm tumblers, churning the black water as the rapid thunder of autofire lanced through the noise of the straining rotors.

The Beretta blew back and locked empty as Bolan emptied the clip across the Plexiglas. The jerky movements of the helicopter let him know he'd scored somewhere on the pilot. He reloaded, checking to see that the police boat was coasting to a sideways stop near Keller. His teeth chattered as he made himself swim toward the patrol boat, knowing he had no choice about his destination. Reaching shore was out of the question.

Somebody on board the boat unleashed a .50-caliber deck gun, and green tracers flamed across the snow-flurried night as they tracked the retreating helicopter. The chopper didn't attempt to reengage, and vanished amid the towering buildings before the police gunner could get on track.

Leathering the Beretta, Bolan swam toward the patrol boat, its whirling lights laying down alternating patterns of scarlet and black across the lake. The Klaxon continued its mournful wailing. He overtook Keller before she could pull herself up the ladder rungs one of the policemen had extended. Pulling and pushing, they got her into the boat and a parka-wearing cop threw a heavy blanket over her shoulders.

As the Executioner pulled himself up, he came face-to-face with two .38 service revolvers held by policemen. He paused, shivering with the cold.

"Easy does it, buddy," one of the cops said, waving him up. "We want to get you out of the water, but we're going to do it on our terms."

"What are you doing?" Keller demanded, trying to push her way to his side. The policeman nearest her reached around quickly and snared her, grabbing the blanket, then held her back. She continued to struggle. "He's on your side, dammit."

The cops ignored her outburst. Bolan stepped up, taking care to keep his hands as far away from his body as he could manage. The no-nonsense glare in the five pairs of eyes watching him was warning enough. As soon as he made the deck somebody produced a set of handcuffs and secured his hands behind his back. Then his weapons were taken, leg cuffs and a blanket added.

A grizzled policeman wearing a yellow slicker stepped forward. "You're being remanded to our custody for the duration, mister," he said in a gruff voice, "until we figure out whether or not to bring charges against you for obstructing Chicago police officers in their sworn duty."

Bolan remained impassive. Playing a third side in a two-sided war had been a losing proposition from the start, but it had been the only game in town.

"I wouldn't count on your Fed buddy to bail you out of this one," the man added. "He's not going to know where you are until we make this city safe again.''

"What about the safety of the next city?" Bolan asked quietly. "What about the one after that?"

"It's not our problem, goddammit. We've shed our blood for this."

"What about me?" Keller demanded.

The cop turned away from Bolan and looked at her. "You'll be remanded into custody with him."

"Why? So I can't tell anyone you've got him?"

"No, you're going in as an accessory."

"I'm a reporter."

"Can you prove that?" The man's face was hard and unflinching.

The fight drained from Keller's features. "My purse went down with the helicopter."

"Then, until you can convince us of who you are, I guess we'll have to take you in."

"What about my phone call?"

"You'll get it after you're booked, but I wouldn't hold my breath. It'll take a while to cut to the chase on all of this." The cop walked back to the steering section without another word.

"They can't do this," Keller said, struggling against the men trying to drag her away.

"They already have," Bolan replied. In the east the first reddish tinges of dawn were beginning to touch the sky, but there was no warmth. And time had suddenly run out.

BAREFOOT, AND DRESSED in a gray uniform that was loose in the waist and tight in the chest, Bolan sat on the jail bunk with his back to the wall and his legs crossed in a lotus position. Delaney Keller slept against him, her breath soft and warm against the short hairs of his neck. The long hours she'd been maintaining and the exhaustion of surviving the episode in the lake had drained her.

The cell was standard eight-foot-by-eight-foot issue with steel bars and a depressing atmosphere. The window overlooked a parking lot three stories below, but precious little else of their location was revealed.

Bolan checked his wristwatch. It was only a handful of minutes before nine. The payoff procedures had already begun. He released his pent-up breath slowly through his nose. Things might be over in Chicago, but he wasn't about to let go of it yet.

Footsteps echoed out in the hall, and a lock clicked. Angry voices were pierced by the shrill squeakings of the hallway gate being slid back.

Keller stirred against Bolan's shoulder, snuffling tiredly as she raised a palm to her eyes.

Brognola stepped into view with fire in his eyes. He spoke without looking at the jailer and the two uniformed officers trailing him. "Open that damned door and get him out of there." The head Fed looked worn and empty, his wrinkled tie knotted precisely but losing a lot of the effect. The only thing about him that looked totally fit for active duty was the shiny leather briefcase handcuffed to his wrist.

The jailer unlocked the door, slid it open and stepped back out of the way. A sour expression covered the flat planes of his face.

"Time to go," Bolan said, uncurling from the bunk and helping Keller to her feet.

"Where are we going?" the reporter asked. She draped the bunk's only blanket around her shoulders.

"Out." Bolan ignored the policemen, wondering how Brognola had been able to cut him free so soon. Things would have been different if they had booked him into the jail and found out who he really was instead of just being concerned with getting him off the street. His fingerprints would have ensured a stay of the permanent sort. Special Agent Fox was trouble, but Mack Bolan was a wanted man.

"The blanket stays in the cell," the jailer said as he reached for it.

Bolan caught the big man's hand and twisted, bringing the jailer's arm in line as he froze the guy into position. "I'll make sure it's mailed back to you or left with the officer who has our personal effects." His voice was soft and graveyard still.

The two uniforms didn't know what to do and reached for their guns hesitantly.

"Don't make this any worse than it already is," Brognola growled. The threat lay heavy in his words. "So far, you people have finally started making some smart moves. Don't screw it up now."

"You're a lucky man, Fox," the jailer said as he took back his hand, massaging it briefly before slamming the door back into place. "The people upstairs don't usually lose paper sent from the White House."

Out in the hallway, at the window waiting for the return of their personal effects, Brognola said, "This is the newswoman?"

Bolan nodded and made the introductions. Keller stuck her hand out from the blanket long enough to shake hands.

"How did you find us?" she asked.

Bolan signed for his box, said, "Later," and stepped aside so the reporter could do the same. He looked over his shoulder and saw half a dozen uniformed men glaring at him. "Didn't really make it on this one with the home team, did we?"

Unwrapping a cigar, Brognola said, "Not hardly. Can't say that I blame them, though. If things were different, if I was still part of a metro squad charged with looking out for my own, maybe I'd have done the same thing. The way they see it, cooling you saved a lot of lives."

"And endangered a lot more," Bolan said as they walked through the hallway.

"How do you figure that?" Keller asked.

"This crew got away with it again." The warrior checked his weapons and made sure the firing pins were in good shape and not "accidentally" broken. Satisfied, he reloaded them, the dry snap of metal against metal loud in the hallway. "They took some losses this time, but they'll come back next time a little wiser, a little more seasoned. They'll kill more hostages later on to up the ante, to show the next city how much closer to the edge they are."

"You make them sound like animals." The thought clearly didn't sit well with Keller. She wrinkled her nose in disgust.

"They're human jackals," Bolan said as they passed through the front door of the small precinct. The cold air hammered into them, whipping Keller's blanket and causing her to yelp as she grabbed for it. "They like the hunt, and they like the taste of blood."

"I've got a car over there." Brognola pointed at the dark sedan parked curbside, and led the way.

Bolan slid in the passenger side, pausing to kick the clumped snow from his bare feet. Keller took a seat in the back and wrapped the blanket tightly around her.

Uncuffing the briefcase, Brognola put it next to Bolan and got in. "Aaron got some prelim intel together," the big Fed said as he dropped the car in gear and merged with the early-morning traffic. "It may tell us who, but we still haven't defined a home base."

Bolan freed the Desert Eagle and tucked it between his knees as he swept his eyes across the streets. "I need to talk to him. I've got a couple things I'd like him to look into. Maybe it'll give us the where."

Shaking his head, Brognola said, "You're too hot. You'd be better off at a neutral base while we push at this thing some more. We're touch and go with the Chicago PD at the moment, even with the Man's paper, and there's the possibility the strike force left a couple of loose guns in town to take care of you. That action over Lake Michigan was definitely geared to take you out of the play. Evidently you got under somebody's skin. They've made you to a degree."

"The action's here, and in all the years you've known me, you've never seen me quit a hot zone until the job was done."

"I know, but I've got some things on a burner that I can't let go of. I don't need the added hassle of having you drawing hostile interest from the friendlies. I do need you near a fax machine so I can get the intel to you as Aaron comes up with it. *If* he comes up with anything. These guys are like phantoms.''

Keller leaned forward and smiled. ''I've got a fax machine at my place.''

Bolan studied the woman, remembering the pluck and courage it had taken for her to get next to him during the operation. There were a lot of things he saw there that he liked, a lot of sand and grit. ''This doesn't mean you'll get everything that I get. You might not even end up with a story.''

''No deals or bargains this time, Fox. Granted, it would make a hell of a story and I'd love to be the one to break it, but seeing these people put away somehow seems a lot more important this morning than a byline.''

Going with the sincerity he sensed in Keller's words, Bolan asked, ''What's the address?''

''MORE COFFEE?'' Keller asked.

Bolan nudged his cup forward and let her pour, pausing to attempt blinking the bleariness from his eyes after reading the files Brognola had left with him.

They sat at the reporter's small breakfast table in a tiny kitchenette, empty plates and manila folders covering the table, extra chairs and the ledge of the picture window overlooking downtown Chicago. Green plants hung from the ceiling in most of the rooms of the two-story town house apartment, while others occupied floor space in brass planters. The neatness of the woman's home had been a surprise, taking into consideration her on-the-run life-style and the seriousness with which she pursued it, marred only by the work area tucked in the second bedroom upstairs where Bolan had found the fax machine.

"Are you okay?" Keller asked as she put the coffeepot to one side.

Bolan focused on her as he considered her question. She looked different in the pink bathrobe, her face scrubbed clean of cosmetics and dirt, and her hair still damp and combed straight back to fall well below her shoulders. "Yeah, I'm just tired."

"You've been going through those reports for over two hours. Maybe you ought to give yourself a break and veg out a little." She stood and started clearing away the breakfast dishes.

Bolan snared a final piece of cold toast and lathered it with grape jelly before she took it away. He was surprised by the passage of time, surprised at the way he'd felt comfortable with the woman despite the limited amount of conversation she'd been able to force out of him while he studied the intel Kurtzman had amassed. He noticed how Keller looked in the bathrobe and quickly realigned his thinking.

"It's different with you, isn't it?" she asked when she returned to sit at the table.

He closed the file he had open before him. "What?"

"This situation. Chicago is going to go through the moves of trying to follow up on this, but basically they're just beating their chests and licking their wounds. By this time next week, everything will be back to business as usual."

"Not quite," he said. "There'll be a lot of ghosts haunting the city for a long time. There'll be people who never get over what happened to them because they know what really went down.''

"It was a holdup,'' she said. "On a larger scale than anything I've ever seen before, but it was still robbery.'' A sad smile played with the corners of her mouth. "Western movies thrived on this sort of thing, remember? The Dalton gang would ride in, shoot up the town, and Roy Rogers would bring them all to justice in between prairie songs.''

"Where is the justice here?''

"There isn't any, really, but the people who survived this unhurt are going to tell themselves there is, and they'll get on with their lives. What choice do they have?''

"They could beard the lion in its den and make sure it never comes out again.''

"Most people aren't trained for that kind of thing,'' she replied. "Even the police departments weren't a match for them.''

"And these people had a lot more taken away from them than money. How many are going to feel truly safe in their homes again? How many are going to wake up in the middle of the night sure that—somewhere—it's happening all over again?''

Keller didn't say anything as she wrapped her arms around herself.

"People believe in the intangible things in life. They believe in the future, security, that you can pull yourself up by your bootstraps, and somewhere in there, justice. Without believing in those things, where would we be? You force yourself through the bad days by telling yourself tomorrow will be better, even though there are no guarantees. How do you think you'd manage if you thought tomorrow could be even worse?"

"I couldn't."

Bolan paused, lost in the memories for a moment. "Justice is something I choose to believe in, and that belief has been sorely tried from time to time. But I cling to it. And if the pursuit of it transcends state or international boundaries, and if I have to help it along, I've never hesitated. I never will. Sometimes we forget that it was only through the efforts of others that we even have those things to believe in, and the whole concept becomes a myth."

"So you choose to defend the myth?"

"I choose to defend the reality."

She studied him, not letting him know the thoughts that cycled behind the dark eyes. "I've never met anyone like you," she said finally, "and it makes me sad to think I'll probably never get to know you completely."

The phone rang shrilly, shattering the silence that built up between them. Bolan took the opportunity to reopen the file and shelve the feelings the woman's proximity stirred within him.

Keller picked the receiver up from the bar, spoke briefly, then held it out to him with her hand over the mouthpiece. "Someone named Aaron?"

"That's the call I've been waiting for." Bolan stood and headed for the stairs. "I'll take it up here." Seconds later he picked up the extension in the office, said hello and listened as the woman hung up.

"Sorry I couldn't get back to you sooner, Mack," Kurtzman said, "but Hal and I have been busy arranging a secure line to do business over. And it took a little longer to assemble the data than I'd anticipated. Still a lot of red tape over there since the Wall came tumbling down."

"I read you. What have you got for me?"

"Get your fax machine warmed up. I'm going to be sending some pictures across first, then I'll get to the debrief."

Bolan switched on the machine and connected the phone, watching silently as pictures and data began streaming out of it. He collated and flipped through them, familiarizing himself with the organization. When the fax machine hummed to a stop, he lifted the receiver to his ear again.

"The guy you're looking for is definitely Konrad Dreyse," Kurtzman said. "One of the guys you put down at the warehouse checked back to Dreyse during his South African merc days."

"I take it the West Germans weren't happy about revealing they had a viper in the nest."

"Officially the guy doesn't exist. Unofficially I know some people who shoot straight and realize the problem we're dealing with here. Dreyse got his counterterrorism training through Grenschutzgruppe 9, and was a promising young officer from all accounts."

Bolan studied the top picture, seeing a young man dressed in what looked like a Federal Republic of Germany border patrol uniform. Only the narrow badge of the German eagle flanked by oak leaves differed from the standard uniform issue.

"This proves your guess about the Volkswagen vans was on the money."

"What pulled him into the merc business?"

"He had nowhere else to go at the time. Dreyse was busted out of GSG-9 a few years ago for arranging evacuations of East German families from Berlin for a price. He'd assembled his own little core group of military people from GSG-9, the border patrol and the German army and gone into business for himself. They did piecemeal work, but it was profitable. It also was bloody more times than not, and the East Germans were building a file on him as well. In fact, it was an East German assassination attempt that blew his cover for the GSG-9 when they lodged a formal complaint and provided pictures."

"So he went to South Africa to market his skills."

"One step ahead of Colonel Uwe Dee's troops. Dreyse earned a reputation over there, too. He was a good tactician, and marshalled the troops that came over with him into a small army as East and West German guards were mustered out of the service and had no place to go after the Wall went down."

"He had a big resource there."

"Yeah. You know the story, Mack. Nobody wants the soldiers around after the war's over."

Bolan knew it only too well.

"Anyway, things got too hot for our boy, and he decided to pull out of the South African front when the Israelis started coming on stronger. Apparently there was a lot of friction there, and he didn't have as much to offer with the way Israel was spreading high-tech hardware around down there."

"Why haven't I ever heard of this guy?"

"You probably have. Dreyse operated under different aliases," Kurtzman said. "That way he could build confidences through dummy names and keep all of his team working. It took a lot of scavenging through files to come up with what I'm able to give you, and I bet I haven't uncovered the half of it. During the Angola crisis, Dreyse had hired out advisory teams to both sides without anyone being the wiser. I got that from a cross-reference into British SAS files. We're dealing with one canny son of a bitch here.''

"So he moved on to the United States."

"Got a wide-open market here for terrorism," Kurtzman commented. "People here aren't used to dealing with it in their backyards."

"I know." Bolan put the papers to one side. "Where is Dreyse now?"

"I haven't got a clue. His trail ends in the files I found a year ago."

Bolan settled back in the swivel chair, letting his thoughts assemble. "Let's chase a couple things and see where they end."

"Shoot."

"How did Dreyse and his team get the Volkswagen vans and the helicopter into Chicago?"

"They could have brought them in a few at a time."

"What about the serial numbers on the engines?"

"The three recovered and documented checked out clean."

"They weren't stolen?"

"No."

"And yet, the numbers were clean."

"Yes. Only the license plates had been switched."

Bolan rubbed his stubbled chin, losing himself in memories of the previous night's action. "Tell me if I'm wrong, but I think all of them were late models."

"They were this year's."

"It would have been a lot of trouble to have stolen vehicles with that kind of history."

"You think they bought them?"

"Yes."

"How?"

"From a dealership, or rather as a dealership. It might be interesting to see what you can find out from U.S. Customs, since those are imports and hit the federal tax sheets."

"I'll get on it now. Shit, I should have thought of something like this. Who else would be in a better position to dump vehicle registrations with no complaints than the company that supposedly sold them?"

"Like you said, this team is well organized and well equipped. The best way to fade into the surroundings is to become part of them. I'm betting Dreyse covered his bases before he ever set foot in Chicago. I think I may have a flash for the IDs of those bodies."

"Give it to me."

"See if any of them are listed with commercial chauffeur's licenses in any of the states that have been hit so far. Eighteen-wheelers come and go every day at all hours. If I was moving a crew in to do the things Dreyse is doing, I'd definitely want to use registered haulers handling the roads."

"I'll get back to you as soon as I find out anything," Kurtzman said.

Bolan broke the connection.

KELLER HESITATED at the bathroom door, the towel Fox had asked for hanging over her arm. Steam covered the glass shower panels and rose in clouds above them. Emotions still whirled dizzily inside her. She'd seen the fax papers lying on her desk unattended and had been able to walk away without looking at them, something that surprised her to no end. Now, looking at the shadowy image of the man on the other side of the shower panels, she received another surprise when desire flooded through her.

Fox was darkly handsome, rugged and lean, but there was more to her feelings than the man's appearance. She'd seen him in operation, seen him battle valiantly in the face of danger, and had sensed that he'd lived one heartbeat ahead of death for a long time.

"You've got a genetic weakness for underdogs, long shots and inside straights," she whispered to herself in anger. "And stray cats." Giving in to impulse, she quickly stripped off her clothing, slid the shower door open and stepped inside. She tried a smile when he looked at her, but it felt false. When he continued to eye her dispassionately, her cheeks burned and she wondered if there was any way she could back out of the situation gracefully. The water sluiced against her, spraying into her eyes as it splattered from his shoulders. "Maybe this wasn't a good idea," she said as she fumbled for the panel.

He touched her arm gently and pulled it back from the door.

She looked up at him and noticed for the first time that those hard eyes could twinkle. "It wasn't just me feeling it, was it?"

He shook his head and grinned. "Not by a long shot."

"A long shot," she repeated as she stepped into his embrace. Scars covered his body, a flesh-and-blood tour of past duty served to the causes that motivated him.

He lifted her chin with a forefinger and kissed her.

Goose bumps covered her as she returned it. His touch was more gentle than she'd imagined, and he seemed hesitant to rush the encounter, wanting to take his time getting to know her body. Anxious, knowing they didn't have much time to share, she wrapped her legs around his waist, closing her eyes as he slid into her and started pushing her toward the edge of an orgasm. The tile felt cold against her back as he leaned her into it and kept moving. She didn't mind at all.

BOLAN SNARED the telephone beside the bed before the second ring, cradling the receiver to his ear as Keller stirred to wakefulness against his chest. "Go," he directed.

"You were right about the Volkswagens," Kurtzman said. "There's a three-month-old dealership in Chicago missing twelve units from their lot. When Brognola got there, the place was closed down and no one responded to the B.I.D. numbers when the PD tried to call."

"Probably figured things were too hot and pulled out of town," Bolan agreed. "Who owned the dealership?"

"A guy who only exists on paper. But I did find out the shipment originated in Seattle, Washington, at a dealership that's been in business for less than a year. This same Washington dealership handled vehicle transfers to Dallas and San Francisco during the time periods we're looking at. As a bonus, one of the guys you took down at the warehouse had a commercial chauffeur's license and is listed as a driver for the Washington end, not under the name on the ID he had on him."

"Where does Washington lead?" Bolan asked. "It doesn't scan that Dreyse can house his operation there. We're looking for someplace more secluded."

"I haven't found anything yet, but maybe you can shake something out of Washington."

"There's a Lear waiting on me at—"

"The guy's already filed a flight plan."

"Does Hal know?"

"He's standing down. Can't make the jump with you yet because he's still smoothing ruffled feathers in Chicago, but he's ready to provide whatever assistance you need. If you can find these guys, it'll probably cut through a lot of the bullshit he's wading in."

"I'll call you the minute I get anything," Bolan said. "One other thing."

"Name it."

"There's a reporter named Keller at this number. Whenever the cover's pulled off this operation, I want her to have a jacket a couple hours before the press releases. She's got a thing for exclusives."

Keller smiled, but there was a sadness in her eyes.

"This the same lady who helped pull you out of the fire at Soldier Field?"

"Yeah."

"Hal already had her down as a release source. I've been assembling Special Agent Fox's bio for print, and built in a few false leads that will keep anyone from putting two and two together."

"Take care of her for me." Bolan broke the connection and put the phone away.

"You didn't have to do that, you know. I didn't cut you any easy deals last night, and if you think you owe me something because of this morning—"

Bolan placed a forefinger over her lips. "I don't feel that way at all. I just know you'll do a fair job." He eased out from under her, regretting losing the warm feel of feminine flesh. She pulled the covers tightly around her and watched him dress.

"Will I see you again?" she asked as she slipped out of bed and pulled on her robe.

"I don't know." Bolan buckled on the damp leather containing the Desert Eagle. "My line of work doesn't allow me to make a lot of promises like that."

She embraced him and pressed her head to his chest. "Just promise me you will if you ever have the chance."

Bolan kissed the top of her head. "You've got my word on it."

Turning, he left and headed out of the apartment without a backward look.

"BOLAN!"

The Executioner froze before opening the sedan Brognola had left for his use, lifting his hands away from his sides. "This is getting to be a habit, Trebeck."

"You made me?" the detective asked as he stepped around to face Bolan, the .357 in both hands before him. "I guess I shouldn't be surprised. You've got a rep for knowing what goes on around you."

Bolan studied the man, seeing the weariness that had gone almost soul-deep.

"Why did you come this way if you knew I was out here?" Trebeck said.

"To give you the chance to say what was on your mind." Bolan dropped his arms to his sides to keep from attracting attention.

The gun jerked in Trebeck's hands. "You take a lot of chances."

"No more than I have to."

"I blamed you for Jack's death."

"I know. I'd have saved him if it was possible, but it wasn't."

"Took me a while to see it that way." Trebeck put the Magnum away. "I heard a whisper about your being connected to the government a while back, but your trial down in Texas seemed to throw that out the window."

"I've still got an occasional friend left, and I've got ways of getting around bureaucracy when I need to."

"I've heard stories. People have told me when you were busting the Mafia's balls, you'd sometimes walk into the middle of a cop head-shed and start calling the shots." Trebeck took a deep breath. "Listen, I followed you from the lockup this morning and sat out here all day freezing my ass off because I figured you'd get a lead on the sons of bitches that hit us last night. I'm here because I want in."

"No," Bolan said flatly. He opened the car door.

Trebeck put a hand out and stopped it. "I want in," he repeated.

"The last thing I need is someone working this thing who's personally involved."

"Way I heard it, that's how you got your start, homeboy. The way I see it, it takes somebody who's personally involved to see these things through to the end. Jack was my partner and my friend.''

"Leave it alone. It'll get taken care of.''

"By who? The only person I see doing any moving around here is you. Brognola's still involved with the politicians downtown. Who else you got backing your play, my man? Everybody knows you work solo.''

Bolan didn't say anything.

"You were the joker in the deck," Trebeck went on. "Somebody slipped you in without the home team figuring out who you really were. Now your ass is hanging out there all by its lonesome until you get something to work on because nobody wants to hang with you. Now, we either play ball together, or I'm going to take in one of this nation's most wanted fugitives. I'm not going to let the chance of hitting back at these bastards die with you.''

Remembering another time long ago when a young soldier came home to bury his family and found a need inside himself to prevent the same thing from happening to other families, Bolan nodded. There was no way he could try to talk Trebeck out of taking an active part one way or the other. He looked at the detective and asked, "Have you ever been to Seattle?''

10

Still operational under the Fox ID, Mack Bolan walked across the showroom floor of the Seattle Volkswagen dealership with the appearance of a bored man doing a boring job. A salesman with a too-wide smile approached him immediately. The warrior came to a halt at the front fender of a red sports car and waited, taking in the five other salesmen working the showroom. Considering the time was 8:00 p.m., the numbers were impressive. And the coats were carefully tailored.

"May I help you, sir?" the salesman asked. He stopped far enough away to be out of easy reach.

Combat senses tingling, Bolan produced his FBI credentials and flashed them. "Could I speak to the manager?"

"I'll get him," the salesman said and walked back toward the desk.

The bell on the entrance doors tinkled again and Trebeck, wearing street clothes and a long black leather coat, stepped into the room, his eyes hidden by mirror sunglasses that stood out against his dark face. His smile was white and dazzling as he ran his palm along the lines of the white convertible on the other side of the showroom. He whistled appreciatively.

Bolan glanced at the Chicago detective and could tell by the man's stance that he'd picked up the warning vibes as well. They didn't talk much during the flight. Trebeck seemed uncomfortable with the way he'd forced himself into Bolan's camp, while the warrior had studied his unexpected partner and reflected on the file Brognola had provided on the man. Trebeck was walking a fine line between conscience and duty, trapped between guilt and failure, and the only way Bolan had ever found to combat those feelings was on the battlefield. The problem was, this particular hell zone might get too hot and cost Trebeck his life before it was over.

The salesman reached the desk and spoke briefly to the man behind the counter, then turned and smiled at Bolan as the counterman reached for something.

The Executioner freed the Desert Eagle from the pocket of his trench coat as the counterman came up firing a mini-Uzi. He dropped the .44 into target acquisition as 9 mm parabellums tore through the sheet metal of the sports car with a blaze of thunder that made hearing impossible. The first 240-grain round took the shooter just below the throat, throwing him backward even as the second round crunched into his face just below his nose. The corpse sank down and disappeared behind the counter.

Sustained bursts of gunfire came from Trebeck's position, letting Bolan know the man had unlimbered the MAC-10 he'd carried in under the coat. Windshield glass scattered over the Executioner's head as he dived behind the sports car and slid along the tiled floor.

As Bolan rolled out to extend the Desert Eagle toward the first salesman, who now clenched an H&K pistol in his fist, he saw two of the other men go down under the assault from Trebeck's MAC-10. He aimed the .44 over the salesman's heart and triggered two rounds in quick succession as the man fired at Trebeck. The hollowpoints took the guy in the chest and staggered him back with quick, shuddering steps to land in a heap over a potted plastic bush.

Bolan's eyes swept the area, searching for the fifth man. A glimmer of movement to his right drew him to his feet as a short burst from an Uzi scarred the floor where he'd been. Reaching under the trench coat, he tugged a grenade off his combat harness and flipped it toward the two men who'd come out a side door. The explosion put one of the men down and ripped holes in the side of a nearby luxury van, rocking it on its wheels. The Executioner's follow-through on the remaining man caught the gunner as he planted his feet and locked the Uzi on full-auto.

Sparks screamed from the concrete pillar beside Bolan as he returned fire. The body hurled backward to crash through a plate glass office window. Bolan reloaded as he surveyed the carnage that had become of the showplace. No longer did the air reek of the smell of new cars. Clouds of gray cordite snaked among the unbroken fluorescent tubes covering the ceiling.

"Trebeck," Bolan called, covering the open space with the .44 in a Weaver stance as he moved cautiously. Wind rushed through the broken display window and the sounds of traffic echoed inside the showroom.

"Here." Trebeck stood up, the MAC-10 cradled in his arms.

"The last man?"

"Down."

Bolan nodded and moved toward the back of the building. A hallway behind the counter led to a series of small, glassed-in offices, each with its own plastic tree. He secured the doorway before entering, letting Trebeck back him up. "You check that side," the warrior said, indicating the left bank of offices, then headed into the first office on the right.

"What are we looking for?" Trebeck asked as he shouldered the MAC-10 and drew the .357.

"Shipping invoices." Bolan opened the filing cabinet in the office, riffling files and throwing them on the floor. "Particularly ones for the Volkswagen vans' serial numbers on that list I gave you, and anything else you find that doesn't seem to fit." Finished with the top drawer, he moved to the next. Folders spilled from his hands, containing sales agreements, warranties and applications. Apparently the dealership had done some real business as well as being a front for Dreyse's vehicular needs.

Ten minutes later Bolan was working his third office and caught the far-off strains of an approaching siren.

"We really should have checked in with the local people before pulling this," Trebeck said.

"We would've lost too much time. These guys were waiting on us or anyone who got this close. By the time we got a raid set up through the Seattle PD and moved with it, they could have notified Dreyse we'd made it this far. All we can hope for now is that Dreyse hasn't been able to completely cover his tracks."

"What if he picks up and leaves?"

"The operation's too big for that."

"Hey, I think I've got something."

Bolan left the office, hearing the squeal of tires slide to a stop in front of the showroom. He looked at the open file Trebeck held, matching the list of serial numbers he had with the ones on the printout. He scanned the information quickly.

Trebeck tapped the middle section. "Looks like the freighter that brought them over made a stop in Alaska." He reached for the telephone. "I'm going to call the locals and let them know we're in the building so they don't shoot us before they read us our rights."

The layover was an island at the end of the Aleutian chain. Thinking of the winter wasteland that occupied that part of the world, Bolan believed Dreyse couldn't have found a more naturally defensible position if he'd tried. And he was sure the man had.

THE COMMANDER of SEAL Team 6 stuck his pipe in his mouth before speaking. He faced Bolan directly, eyes hard and direct. The uniform and the man seemed to consist of hard edges and sharp, crisp angles. "You realize what we're talking about here couldn't even have been done if relations between the United States and Russia hadn't lightened up."

"I know. That's why we're doing it this way, and why we're letting Soviet forces know we're going to have that kind of hardware in the area." Bolan poured himself another cup of coffee and remained standing. "Dreyse was counting on the proximity of the two countries being diversionary and constraining when he set up his base there."

Besides Bolan, there were three men in the small office at the Navy Amphibious Warfare School in Coronado, California. Hal Brognola took up a seat at the long table in the center of the room. Brent Walthers was the representative of the Joint Special Operations Command, who maintained a vested interest in the counterterrorist activities of SEAL Team 6.

Commander Will Traven smiled slightly. "You sound like you've got this guy pegged as one crafty son of a bitch, Fox."

Bolan held up three fingers. "He's taken down three cities hard, Commander. Do you know anybody else who's been able to do that?"

"No."

"Dreyse is good," Bolan went on. "You need to know that before we ever weigh anchor, otherwise you're going to lose a lot of your men, and maybe allow Dreyse to run and fight again another day."

Traven shook his head. "You'll never see the day that happens. My people have been trained and trained hard to take care of this kind of situation. You won't find anyone better."

"I know," Bolan said. "That's why I asked that SEAL Team 6 be assigned to this."

The statement caused Traven to lift an eyebrow. "It's interesting to me how a civilian could swing that much support from the Joint Special Operations Command."

Bolan sipped his coffee, knowing the friction he felt between them was the result of two military men used to being in control of whatever assignment was handed them. Even knowing it, as he was sure Traven did as well, he found he couldn't free himself of the automatic responses of mental push and shove.

"Rest assured, Commander Traven," Walthers interrupted, "Special Agent Fox has all the authority he needs. Or do I need to remind you whose signature was on the orders you were cut?"

"No, sir. It's just that I'm used to calling my own shots. I find it uncomfortable to be placed under civilian advisement."

"However, Commander, in this case that's where you are," Walthers said.

"Yes, sir."

Ignoring the presence of the Joint Special Operations Command man, Bolan focused on Traven. "Look, I've been actively tracking Dreyse for some time now, even before we had a name on the guy, and I've got a little insight to how he thinks. I studied the surface layout of his operation on Hobbes Island for the past three hours while your team was arriving. I've put together an assault plan, and you're free to make whatever revisions you feel are necessary, but we're running out of time. I considered a solo penetration mission, but it's not the man who's the threat. It's the operation itself. Dreyse did a good job, his people are well-researched and well-trained. You could cut off the head of one serpent and a new one would instantly take over. I want to take it all down."

Traven's look was cool and appraising. "You think you could have done it?"

"I wasn't always an FBI agent," Bolan replied truthfully.

Traven didn't appear to be convinced. "I had your jacket pulled on the flight over here, Fox, as well as the reports of what went down in Chicago. I wasn't impressed. According to what I read, you may be held responsible for the deaths of a lot of good men in that town."

"Commander Traven!" Walthers's outburst was an explosion as he shoved his chair back.

Brognola grabbed the man's arm and guided him back to his seat with a quiet admonishment to stay out of things for the moment.

"There's a terrorist cell operating within and against the United States," Bolan said quietly, "and they're going down tonight with you in charge of your unit or not. That's your decision."

Traven stared at him for a moment, then looked at Walthers. The Joint Special Operations Command rep nodded. "One thing's for damn sure, mister, my team isn't going in without me."

"I wouldn't want them to," Bolan replied.

"Let's take a took at this tactical op you say you've developed."

Brognola switched off the lights and the projector light flashed across the white screen as Bolan put up the first picture Kurtzman had provided. It was an aerial, far enough out so the outlines of the buildings below were vague and fuzzy, yet showed an overview of the frozen surface of the island complex. "This is Dreyse's cover," Bolan said without checking the notes that had accompanied the presentation. The information had been committed to memory hours ago. He walked to the screen and telescoped a pointer between his hands.

Traven took a seat away from the table.

"This is the main building," the warrior stated, indicating the large structure to the southeast corner. "According to our intel, Dreyse operates a shipping business here under the name Joel Dawes. The cover was a professional one, but since we knew what we were looking for going in, it didn't stand up at all." He traced the dirt roads leading to the dock area and the other buildings. "Satellite observation leads us to believe he maintains well over a hundred men on base once everyone's in position, and that figure may be low. Once we're grounded, we could be up against as many as two hundred trained soldiers."

"Is anyone else on this island?" Traven asked.

"No. Everyone living there is connected in some way to Dreyse. Under the Dawes name, his people do maintainence work on drilling sites around Alaska, and have even done work on the pipeline project. They also operate an emergency repair service for ocean-going vessels that helps explain all the communications equipment to the ships passing through. He moved into this area almost four years ago, while he was still involved in the merc business in Africa, and gradually went into business."

"You're saying this man was planning this as long as four years ago?" Walthers asked. The disbelief showing on the man's face told Bolan that the guy hadn't read the file he'd prepared closely, if at all.

"That's exactly what I'm saying. Dreyse has been an opportunist from the beginning. That's why he's set up as well as he is now. This island is an armed encampment with the latest in high-tech gear." Bolan tapped two buildings on either side of the warehouse.

"Since recon started on the island last night, it's been discovered that these two buildings house Stinger shoulder missiles capable of taking out either an air or water aggressor."

"They have radar?" Traven asked.

"And sonar. This is one well-equipped battle station." Bolan clicked the projector button and flipped through the slides as he spoke. "The troops are quartered here, in the building directly behind the warehouse. Notice the outbuildings and how they're staggered to permit recovery action during an attack." He stopped on a close-up. "They're also equipped with snipers."

The scene changed, showing a bleak outcrop of frozen rock directly behind the barracks. "Satellite recon during the past few hours has also determined the existence of minefields on the north and west sides of the island. Provided you could get men through that without being discovered, they would still have to negotiate that hunk of rock."

"So you're suggesting the only route open to a beach landing is the south and east sides of the island," Traven said. "That will put us directly under fire from the Stinger missiles you say they have."

"By the time your team gets there, the missile sites will be neutralized."

"By who?"

"Me."

"You think you're that good?"

"Yeah."

Traven appeared about to say something but held his comment back. "You plan on doing this by yourself?"

"I want three men, you pick them, to assist me in a standard two-by-two on the buildings. I don't expect this to be clean, but it doesn't have to be as long as those missiles are put down."

"We could send in most of the team the same way."

Bolan shook his head. "Remember, these are trained people you're putting your men up against, and we're operating on their home territory. This isn't the same as putting down a bunch of nationals attempting an embassy coup. If we're going to have an edge at all, it's going to mean going in there in a full-scale blitz." He flipped to the next slide. "The outer perimeter is sealed off by an electrically charged fence as well as guard dogs." Another slide came into view, showing an airstrip. "Our intel confirms two C-130 transport planes on the island as well as a Lear. There are going to be Top Gun fighters standing by to intercede if it becomes necessary, but our objective is to put everyone down before a plane has a chance to get into the air. They may try to pull out with evidence, and we need everything we can get, because a few top people in Washington have laid their careers on the line to get us this far this quietly. Everything's got to be nice and neat, and in one package."

"How the hell did this guy get this set up without anyone knowing?" Walthers asked.

Bolan looked at the politician. "Until recently, the United States and the Soviet Union have been too busy watching each other to watch one guy going into business for himself."

Traven leaned forward and knocked the ash out of his pipe, then repacked it. "So how are we going to take this island?"

Bolan told him.

MINUTES BEFORE the *Spearfish* was due to drop anchor outside the reach of the sonar on Hobbes Island, Bolan left the conning tower and made his way through the nuclear submarine to the quarters he'd been assigned. The insulated black diving gear he was to wear during the assault hung beside the bed, his personal armament, webbing and combat harness arranged under it.

He changed clothes, letting his fingers go through the familiar motions automatically as he went over the details in his mind one more time. Someone knocked on the door as he pulled on the heavy neoprene shirt. "Come in."

Trebeck stepped into the room, wearing a suit identical to Bolan's, his wiry hair glittering with moisture. He seemed uneasy. "Looks like it's almost show time," the detective commented dryly.

"Yeah."

Trebeck hooked a finger inside his collar and pulled at it. "You're a hard man to talk to, Bolan. Anybody ever tell you that?"

Bolan tied his boots together and deposited them in the backpack he'd carry until they established the beach operations. "A few times, but generally I thought it was because the other person was uncomfortable with the subject matter."

"You really get right down to it, don't you?"

"I try to."

"Yeah, well, I've been doing some thinking about how I got myself invited to this little dance, and the reasons I did it. It didn't take me long to realize you could've had me removed from the scene by some of your Feeb buddies long before I ever got this far. Instead, you had Brognola clear my being here by saying I was needed to ID some of the terrorists. What I want to know is why you let me get this far."

"Why are you here?" Bolan countered. "Have you asked yourself that?"

Trebeck turned away. "I told myself it was because of Jack, because somebody needed to show those bastards they couldn't just walk into my city, off somebody and walk away. But after the scene in Seattle, after we shot those people instead of playing by the rules I got handed to me when I got my shield, I started wondering about that myself. Got to where I wondered so much I started chasing myself around inside my head."

"Have you got it worked out for yourself yet?"

"I don't know."

"The need for revenge isn't just something you turn on and off," Bolan said. "It's just an emotion that fills you during a traumatic time and takes the pain away and allows you to keep functioning when all you want to do is curl up somewhere and die."

Trebeck faced him. "I know what happened to your folks. It was all in the files. If I'm out of line, tell me. But why are you here?"

"Because I can do something. I've been a soldier most of my life, fighting in one war or another. When I got back from Vietnam, I was forced to look with an adult's eyes at this country I love and had been fighting for. I saw a war going on here, one that no one else seemed to even notice. And I looked at that war like a soldier, with an 'us' and a 'them,' and decided I wasn't bound by the rules that hamstrung the law-enforcement people. Nobody seemed to be taking care of the 'us,' so I started.''

''Yeah, but the rules have got to stand for something.''

''As long as they stand anywhere but in the way, I'm all for them. You're talking about dealing with morality, Trebeck, and part of the morals you've been indoctrinated with say you have to stand for the rules. All my life, I've been trained to stand for the people who couldn't fight for themselves.''

''Would you understand it if I told you shooting those guys back there in Seattle didn't feel right?''

''Yes.''

''Then why am I here?''

''Because you needed to know you weren't letting Jack or yourself down, and I saw the chance of a good cop going down the tubes as a victim of a misplaced guilt. Take a minute to think about how many guys would do the kind of job you do, would voluntarily see the kinds of tragedies you witness every day, and would try to make something good happen of what's left over.''

Trebeck was silent.

''Rules are there as a system of checks and balances,'' Bolan said, ''and we all base ours a little differently. We make compromises every day, and most of them with ourselves. It hurts sometimes, but we go on. If it's any consolation, the compromise you made in coming with me is probably easier than the one you would have made by staying home. This is your first taste of war. A lot of guys I've known have asked the same questions of themselves as you are.''

"Even you?"

"Yeah, especially me, I think."

Trebeck held out his hand and Bolan took it. "Thanks for your time."

The Executioner reached for the rest of his gear as the door closed behind the man.

BOLAN TROD WATER as the three SEALs accompanying him came up out of the Swimmer Delivery Vehicle they'd used to travel from the *Spearfish*. He took the night glasses from his chest pack and scanned the coastline. They'd halted the minisub three hundred yards out, where it could be used by the backup teams from the boat to get to shore.

The water was cold around him despite the insulated clothing, fins and gloves, but the snow-covered topography of the island looked frozen. A darting movement caught his attention and he focused the binoculars on it, bringing the figure closer until he could see it was a man on a snowmobile. An assault rifle hugged the seat under his leg.

Satisfied their approach had gone undiscovered, Bolan put the night glasses away, fit the mouthpiece of the tanks to his teeth and slipped under the dark waters, followed immediately by his team. He swam and conserved his movements, working against the drag of the chest pack and backpack and the watertight case containing the M-16/M-203 conversion he'd chosen as his lead weapon. Speaking through the UTEL microphone embedded in his face mask, Bolan said, "Harrison and Chambers, make your split now, then wait for my signal. Cook, you're on me."

Long minutes later, Bolan and Cook were lying on their stomachs just under the ocean's surface. The warrior removed his face mask so light wouldn't be reflected from the glass, then stuck his head up, relishing the taste of fresh air even though the chill of it almost seared his lungs. He kicked off his fins and let them float away. The icy sensation of the water became worse.

Cook surfaced beside him, water trickling from his face. With the M-16 in his arms now, and the chest pack and backpack loosely hooked to his webbing, the warrior moved in slowly, the assault rifle scant inches above the ocean's surface.

There were no lights in either of the target buildings around the warehouse, and shadows spread outward from the security lights mounted in the rear. The blatting sound of a snowmobile engine broke the silence of the night and rolled over the docking area.

Crawling through what felt like frozen mud, Bolan studied the front of the building he'd assigned to himself and Cook. Nothing moved. With their faces stained as dark as their clothing, he knew there was little chance of their being seen.

Only ten feet of beach separated them from the skeletal shrubbery and pines that clung to the island in scattered clumps.

Cook was a trained professional, and Bolan could almost sense the man stepping in the tracks he'd just left. Slinging the M-16 over his shoulder, the warrior drew the silenced Beretta. Beside him, poised in the last clump of foliage between them and the outbuilding, Cook cocked a crossbow and slid a short bolt home.

Bolan raced across the snow-covered expanse, driving his legs hard, feeling his feet crunch through the frozen layer of ice. He leaped up on the wooden porch that fronted the building, the 93-R leading the way. The rapid vibration under his feet told him someone had seen his approach.

He threw himself at the door and ripped the lock from the frame, leveling the Beretta. Light spilled over him as a naked light bulb clicked on overhead.

There was a momentary image of fur and fangs, then the German shepherd hit him chest high, growling and snarling. Ivory teeth snapped for his throat and left hollow smackings in their wake as he fought the animal off, trying to track the 9 mm on the man in the room aiming an H&K G-11 caseless assault rifle at him. He caressed the trigger even as the dog's weight bowled him over, spitting out a 3-round subsonic burst that removed the top of the guy's head.

The warrior went down on his back, trying to hold off the dog. Then the shepherd gave a small yelp and sprawled bonelessly across his chest. Light glinted off the four razor-sharp spines of the crossbow bolt that had sliced through the animal's heart.

Cook trotted up beside Bolan as he got to his feet, another bolt already notched. The SEAL glanced briefly inside, then said, "Good shooting. He the only one?"

The Executioner nodded, raising the Beretta to put a round through the swinging bulb before someone noticed the light. The glass fragments pinged against the wooden floor. Inside, he quickly located the hard outlines of the shoulder-fired Stinger and shrugged into it, stepping back onto the porch with Cook, who was pulling his boots on over dry socks.

"Chambers and Harrison took the other one down," the man said.

Bolan nodded toward the crossbow. "You can put that away. These people are about to be notified that we're here." He pulled on his own footgear, relishing the feel of the dry socks, then aimed the missile at the barracks.

The Executioner rolled with the discharge of the launcher, riding it out, watching, seeing the sudden explosion that rocked the main house. Fire blazed all around the charred and blasted remains. A heartbeat later, the Stinger fired by Chambers or Harrison took out the hangar where the C-130s were stored.

The battle for Hobbes Island was in full swing.

11

The Executioner sidled around the outbuilding he and Cook had taken over, sighting down the barrel of the M-16 at the building farther back and diagonal from his present position. Yellow tracers spun through the air as a sniper on the roof unveiled the big .50-caliber machine gun hidden there. Bullets peeled long splinters from the wall beside Bolan.

He pulled the trigger on the M-203 and felt the grenade leave the barrel with an insistent push. The 40 mm warhead impacted at the juncture of the first and second floors directly below the sniper's position, and tore away enough supports to leave the upper structure warped. The gunner fell, waving his arms and legs in an attempt to regain his balance. A short burst from the M-16 left the body sprawled under the fiery debris that followed seconds later.

Autofire tracked onto Bolan's position as he moved toward the skimpy cover provided by the naked trees. Branches rained down on the warrior as bullets ripped them free of scarred trunks. Cook joined him, firing brief bursts from his M-16.

Pausing to rip his chest pack free, the Executioner plugged electronic detonators into the plastic explosive inside, then swept it toward the building that had housed the Stinger.

"Fire in the hole!" Bolan yelled as he thumbed the detonator and fell to the ground.

The earth seemed to shake when the C-4 touched off. Dirt, snow, wooden slats and chunks of the concrete foundation vanished during the explosion, then tumbled to the ground moments later.

"They must've had a goddamned arsenal in there," the SEAL yelled above the repercussions of the detonation.

Bolan consulted his watch, found that five minutes had elapsed since the initial explosion that he'd told Traven would be the signal to move in. In another five minutes the first ranks of the SEAL units in the other SDVs that had ridden piggyback on the *Spearfish* would hit the beach, followed in short order by the raft teams. All they had to do was stay alive and provide some kind of diversion that would give the beachhead crews a chance.

The angry buzz-saw roar of an approaching snowmobile cut through the aftereffects of the explosion, interspersed with the harsh bleatings of Klaxons. Concealed lights, more than the satellite and upper altitude recons had warned of, came to life in a brilliant glow that cast twisted and broken shadows across the frozen surface of the island.

Bolan pushed himself to his feet and tracked the sounds of the snowmobile, realizing that it wasn't just one vehicle anymore. He jogged northeast, circling around the perimeters of the lighted area and the buildings, conscious of the SEAL behind him and the movements of Dreyse's troops.

He raced through a spiked tangle of naked and broken branches, diving as the first of the snowmobiles turned in his direction. Blood warmed his cheek from a deep scratch below his right eye, creating a smear as he brought the M-16 into target acquisition.

Dreyse's outer perimeter guards wore white snowsuits that matched the almost blinding glare under the high-intensity security lights. The snowmobile hurtled at the Executioner, bouncing across the uneven ground, the driver looking grim-faced behind the black goggles.

A controlled burst from Bolan's M-16 tracked across the snowmobiler's face, jerking the guy's head back and forth as the 5.56 mm tumblers smashed the body from the seat. Autofire drove the warrior from his position as the numbers continued dropping through his head. His inner sights were set on Dreyse, and he refused to be deterred from his target.

He ran, pumping his legs hard, the powdery layer of snow overlaying the ice making him slip and slide and nearly lose his balance. A lone pine tree towering over a ridge twenty yards away put him closer to the main house and provided shelter, if the two snowmobiles zipping up behind didn't overtake him first. He caught Cook in the periphery of his vision, a half step behind, the SEAL's lungs throwing out gray clouds of vapor.

The meaty smack of bullets striking flesh told Bolan the SEAL had been hit even as they rounded the pine tree together. He reached back, found a one-handed grip on the Navy man's black uniform, and fell backward behind the tree, yanking Cook clear with him. The first snowmobile rushed by as he scrabbled through the frozen snow for his M-16.

The skis locked as the driver struggled to bring the vehicle around, spraying up a glistening white-blue sheet of snow behind him.

Bolan used the color of the flying snow to silhouette his target and let loose a figure eight that emptied the assault rifle's clip and the snowmobile's seat. Before he could load the M-16, the second snowmobile blasted through the other side of the tree, breaking branches in its passage. Acting on reflex, the Executioner swung the assault rifle by the barrel, catching the guy on the head with enough force to drop him out of the saddle.

The Desert Eagle cleared leather as the gunner struggled to bring his Uzi into play. A 240-grain hollowpoint ripped through one of the goggle lenses and punched the man to the ground.

Kneeling, Bolan rammed a fresh clip into the M-16 and checked on the SEAL. Liquid glistened across the man's lower abdomen, dark and oily in the uncertain light. "How bad is it?"

"Bad enough," Cook whispered hoarsely. "Figure on playing it out alone from here." He fumbled weakly for his weapon.

Bolan put the M-16 in the SEAL's hands and helped him get his back against the tree. Cook's pallor was almost as startling as the white ends of the broken tree branches near him.

Drawing his Ka-bar, the Executioner moved to the nearest dead man, cut a section of the man's shirt away, then brought it back to Cook and shoved it inside over the holes in his abdomen. "I'd stay."

"I know." The SEAL breathed with effort.

"Stay hard."

Cook nodded. "The only way there is. When you get a chance and things clear up down there, do me a favor and don't forget I'm out here."

Bolan shook the man's hand, then scooped up the M-16, hung it over his shoulder and ran for the nearest snowmobile. He thumbed the electronic ignition to life and accelerated. Needles of ice seemed to hang in the wind and cut into his face. He powered the snowmobile to the top of the ridge, handling with difficulty the harsh thumping it made as it crossed the frozen ground.

Abandoning the vehicle near the top, the warrior pulled out his night glasses and clambered the rest of the way on his stomach, aware of the familiar sounds of war bursting around him. The chill of the ice, snow and rocky ground seemed like a hungry vampire trying to suck the warmth and life from his body.

Below, in the hollow where Dreyse had built his business cover, everything had turned into a seething caldron of confusion. Snowmobiles flitted across the open expanse as the outer perimeter troops gathered in an attempt to hold their base.

He moved on, taking in the ragged strips of fire that still blazed around the hangar and landing area. Three Jeeps congregated in that area, moving in widening circles as the teams searched the wreckage. Independent action of the men on foot was too erratic to be effective despite the obvious efforts made by commanding officers to pull them into a semblance of order.

This was one point where the sheer numbers of Dreyse's terrorist troops worked against them, made them lethargic in response. Given fifteen or twenty minutes more, the warrior had no doubt that the terrorists could secure their area and repel invaders.

However, the members of SEAL Team 6 didn't intend to give them even five minutes more. Bolan flicked his glasses toward the shore, picking up the first few swimmers as they came clambering up out of the dark waves of the Bering Sea. Small-arms fire lighted up the night, punctuated by the heavier booming of portable mortars and M-60s. The Jeeps converged on the shoreline, and the Executioner could see officers rallying their men on from the rear decks. A ragged line formed, running forward to confront the arriving SEALs.

Bolan dropped the night glasses, letting his combat senses guide him. Dreyse was below, somewhere in that tangle of man against man. He repacked the night glasses and went back for the snowmobile. He slung the M-16 over his left shoulder and positioned it so he could sweep it up and into play if necessary.

Gunning the engine, he went up and over the ridge, drawing fire halfway down as some of the terrorists realized the uniform he wore wasn't one of theirs. He ducked, slid and twisted, forcing the snowmobile in the direction he wanted to go, leaving the ground in ragged-ass jumps that ended in kidney-bruising landings. A handful of rounds tore away the top third of the Plexiglas shield in front of him as he leaned out to guide the snowmobile around an ice-covered boulder at the bottom of the incline. The vehicle shimmied and swerved as it sought level ground, almost dislodging him as it tipped abruptly to one side, then righted itself.

Bullets drummed against the left side of the snowmobile. The warrior felt one round bite deep below his left knee, then he had the M-16 up and tracking the small knot of men confronting him. He sprayed a long burst from left to right as he roared toward them. Three of the gunners were knocked down, two of them diving in headlong plunges and losing their weapons.

The snowmobile's skis tangled briefly in the legs of one of the living men, there was the sound of bones breaking, a scream, and he was through them, hunched low over the handlebars and feeling the blood trickling down his leg. A warhead exploded in front of him, and the snowmobile was airborne for a second as he jumped the resulting crater.

The silvery flash of a Lear jet on the airstrip four hundred yards away caught his attention. A Jeep shrieked to a stop near the hangar, and the Executioner recognized Konrad Dreyse as the man swung out of the driver's seat.

The view was suddenly blocked by a two-ton truck that swung in front of Bolan, the driver's face grim as he bore down on the warrior's Arctic Cat. Short bursts ate into the chassis of the snowmobile, sparking when metal hit metal.

Trapped, with no time and no room to maneuver, Bolan watched the chain-covered tires sweep toward him.

TREBECK'S TEETH chattered as he floundered through the dark waves carrying him away from the motor-equipped rubber raft he'd ridden on. The rest of his team was already far ahead of him and seemed to glide through the icy water that wanted to suck him under.

The Franchi LAW 12 he carried was bulkier than the assault rifles most of the SEALs carried, but it came closer to being a familiar weapon. Bandoliers of ammunition crossed his shoulders. Back on the *Spearfish,* he'd felt uncomfortably overdressed, thinking he looked more like Hollywood's version of a Mexican bandit than a Chicago homicide detective.

Now, with the hollow booming of artillery and the short, sharp barks of automatic-weapons' fire all around him, he wondered if he was equipped well enough to just stay alive. He focused on thoughts of Jack, told himself his being here was going to make some kind of difference, even if the only difference was to Detective Joe Trebeck.

He worked his left hand in the Velcro strap that was there to help minimize the shotgun's recoil. A zigzagging line of bullets ripped through the frozen ground to his left. He brought the LAW 12 on-line even as he dodged, triggering two rounds of double-aught buckshot toward the gunner. Both loads caught the man chest-high and blew him off his feet.

"Pretty fair shootin' for a city boy," one of the SEALs commented dryly as he passed.

Trebeck tried to keep up with the man but couldn't maintain his balance on the snow and ice, wondering if he knew the guy or if it was just someone who'd seen him back on the submarine. He fed two more shells into the shotgun, bringing the total back up to five. The .357 hung in shoulder leather under the overlapping bandoliers.

Then an onslaught of white-suited terrorists on foot, riding snowmobiles and loaded in Jeeps tried to overrun their position.

Trebeck felt totally out of his element as he shouldered the shotgun, squeezed off a round at the M-60 gunner riding in back of the Jeep that broke a hole in their offense, following immediately with another when the first didn't have the desired effect. He squeezed off his third round, the pattern catching the gunner high on the shoulder and spinning him out of the Jeep.

The driver attempted to turn and cut back through the line of SEALs only to be overrun by at least three of the black-clad warriors. Then the U.S. Navy owned their first 4WD on Hobbes Island, and the M-60 had a new gunner.

The shotgun roared into his shoulder again and again as he fired it dry. His fingers were cold and felt thick as he jammed more shells into the magazine. He pumped it, added the fifth, and kept moving, carried along now with the tides of battle instead of the ocean waves.

An explosion knocked him off his feet, and he was busy wondering what had caused it when a man came behind him and helped him up.

"Mortar, chum," the SEAL explained. "Keep lying there like that, and they'll lay the next one in the middle of your ass."

Trebeck stuck with the man, running all-out through carnage that until tonight he'd only witnessed on cable news.

An overturned Jeep, its tires still spinning as fire spread along the ground under it, sat in the middle of the clearing between the building and the barracks. Dead men littered the ground, but most of them appeared to be terrorists.

"Son of a bitch," the SEAL cursed vehemently. He slung his weapon and cupped his hands as he turned to call out. "The plane! The plane!"

Trebeck glanced toward the airstrip and saw the Lear taxiing, gaining speed. His cop's instincts told him immediately who was on board. The head rat hadn't even waited for the ship to sink before abandoning it. Then he saw the empty Jeep sitting by the hangar. Knowing the LAW 12's weight would only slow him down, he dropped it and ran.

KONRAD DREYSE reached behind the Jeep's seat and pulled out the fireproof briefcase containing the IDs and account numbers he'd need to withdraw the monies stashed in the Bahamian banks they'd used for the final deposits. He couldn't even guess how many millions were still tucked securely away, but it was surely enough to keep him safe and well provided.

The sounds of battle rolled across the landing strip, urging him on. Keeping one hand on the briefcase and the other on the mini-Uzi hanging around his neck, he sprinted for the Lear, drawing the attention of the crew that had dragged it from the burning hangar. Metal creaked as the top of the structure gave way with a loud whoosh and crashed to the ground.

"Where's Mecklenberg?" Dreyse asked.

"On board," one of the six men standing before him replied. They were dressed in the white uniforms of the outer perimeter guard. Stains, tears and burned plastic covered their clothing, mirroring the sooty patches, blood and abrasions that covered their exposed flesh.

Dreyse smiled a friendly smile as he closed in on them. "You've managed to save the jet. That was good work." He brought up the mini-Uzi and let loose a blistering salvo that cut into the men, their convulsed bodies dancing briefly before dropping to the ground.

Dreyse was over and past them before the last death twitches stilled. He dropped the mini-Uzi as he caught the slender chain of the ramp and climbed aboard the aircraft.

Moltke met him as he stepped inside, the soldier's face ashen. "My God, Konrad, you shot them down in cold blood."

Ignoring the man's outburst, Dreyse sat the briefcase in a seat to one side and started pulling on the door to get it closed. "Help me, Karl." When there was no response, he looked over his shoulder to find Moltke unmoving.

"They would have died for you."

"They did die for me," Dreyse replied, straining against the weight of the door. "Mecklenberg, take off now."

There was no audible reply, but the jet shuddered as the engines kicked into renewed life. The door came up suddenly, shutting and sealing with a hiss. The aircraft bounced as it sped across the uneven surface of the airstrip, gaining speed when it reached the area the ground teams had kept free of ice and snow.

When Dreyse faced Moltke again, the man held a gun in his hand.

"We've done things before this," Moltke said. "We've had blood on our hands many times, but never have we spilled the blood of our own people. A commanding officer should never turn his back on his troops, Colonel, nor should he murder them."

Holding on to the seat for stability, Dreyse shook his head in disbelief. "There's no army out there now, Karl. Only men running for their very lives even as we are."

"And we should have taken as many of them with us as was possible, not killed them."

"You're a fool. Don't you realize the Americans have broken through our subterfuges? They know who we are now. You'd propose to hide an army of fugitives? Where?"

Moltke hesitated.

Dreyse struggled to make his voice more reassuring. "Karl, there's enough money here to make us both very wealthy men."

"There are rules of conduct you have ignored. Never have I seen you so self-centered." Moltke raised the pistol and pointed it directly between Dreyse's eyes. "You used to be a good soldier, Konrad."

Dreyse shook his sleeve knife free even as he stepped inside Moltke's arm. He shoved a finger under the hammer before it could strike the firing pin and blow a hole in the pressurized cabin. The glittering blade raked across his second-in-command's throat, and he used his forearm to hammer Moltke into a seat beside the briefcase.

He smiled as he wiped the knife clean on Moltke's uniform, then picked up the briefcase and looked down as the man's eyes glazed over. "I'm through with being a good soldier, Karl. Now I'm going to be a good millionaire, and no one's going to stop me." He made his way forward to the cockpit, feeling the nose of the Lear edge up as the wings took the wind. He was home free. The thought left him smiling as he took the copilot's seat and watched the edge of the Bering Sea rush up at him.

ABANDONING the snowmobile to the inevitable, Mack Bolan pushed himself free and managed two running steps before the impossibility of controlled motion at that speed overtook him and spilled him across the frozen ground. He got a blurred image of the snowmobile shredding under the chain-wrapped tires, then the gas tank exploded and left a layer of fire clinging to the undercarriage of the truck.

He watched the truck lumber in a half circle as he forced himself to his knees and shouldered the M-16. Triggering the grenade launcher, he put a round into the canopy-covered bed where at least a dozen terrorists had gathered and were trying to bring him into their sights. The 40 mm warhead exploded and flung bodies through the canopy, leaving a warped metal skeleton behind.

The driver brought the truck around with a gnashing of gears. Bolan heard the engine sucking gas as it powered toward him again. He reloaded the M-203, still on his knees, then let the deathbird fly, turning away before it impacted against the nose of the truck and shoved the engine through the men behind it.

Using the M-16 as a cane, the Executioner levered himself to his feet, feeling the weakness in his injured leg but ignoring it. Three men went down under short bursts from the assault rifle as he forced himself to run toward the airstrip.

The Lear was taxiing smoothly now, though unable to get up to speed because it was still on the icy patches of the runway.

Bolan threw down the M-16 a second before he assaulted the ten-foot fence surrounding the hangar area. He grabbed handfuls of the mesh once, twice, threw his injured leg across the top and followed it over, pain shooting through him as the weakened limb threatened not to take the weight. He pushed off with his hands, eyes on the blinking lights of the vanishing jet, catching Trebeck on the periphery of his vision as the detective closed in from the left.

By the time he reached the Jeep, Trebeck slid behind the steering wheel and hit the starter.

"You got any plans on how we're going to work this?" Trebeck asked as he put his foot down hard on the accelerator. The four-wheel drive lunged forward, chains rasping against the ice until they found purchase.

"Catch it first," Bolan said as he seated himself. He shrugged out of his backpack, brought it around in front of him and rummaged through it until he found his last block of C-4 with accompanying detonator.

Cold wind snapped around the Jeep's windshield. The tires skidded on the ice for a moment, causing the 4WD to swerve out of control. Bolan watched the distance between the Lear and the Jeep diminish as he prepared the plastic explosive charge by feel. The receivers shoved in, the warrior tucked the bundle inside his wet suit and pocketed the detonator.

"Get under the wing," Bolan commanded, standing up in the seat. His wounded leg quivered from the strain of fighting the acceleration and the wind resistance.

The jet's engines screamed into renewed life, pulling it away for a moment. The wing slid across Bolan's fingertips, just out of reach.

"You'll never make it, Bolan," Trebeck shouted. "You're committing suicide."

"Get up there, closer to the fuselage." Bolan leaned forward, gritting his teeth against the cold and the pain. He ducked as they passed under the wing, wrapping both hands around the front of it, feeling the material of his gloves rip on the sharp edges.

The Lear became airborne with a suddenness that almost pulled the Executioner's arms from their sockets. He dangled for a moment, pinned by the slipstream against the cold metal, fighting to stay with it as the ground dropped away beneath him. He had a momentary impression of Trebeck skidding wildly out of control, then he looked back up at the wing between his two hands and started hauling himself up.

Taking advantage of the pilot's bank toward the east, the Executioner hauled himself up on the wing, knowing his shifting weight would alert the people inside the aircraft.

Bolan freed the pack of C-4 as a dizzying panorama of black ocean twisted beneath him. A shadow caught his attention as he pounded the plastic explosive into place, overlapping the wing so the air friction that threatened to tear him from the metal skin of the jet would ensure that the C-4 stayed in place.

Konrad Dreyse's face was framed in the window that overlooked the wing. The unbelieving expression on the terrorist's face changed to horror when the Executioner pointed out the plastic explosive. Bolan made a cocking motion with his hand, pulled the imaginary trigger and pushed himself away from the wing, letting the rushing wind take him.

He pushed the detonator button through his pocket and the jet transformed into a brief orange-and-white comet streaking across the star-filled sky.

The drop to the ocean's surface was less than seventy feet. Cold water closed over the warrior and took away the light. He went deep, completely disoriented for a moment, waiting with his lungs near collapse as buoyance showed him the way. He stroked for the surface, not hurrying his movements, wanting to conserve his energy to make sure he made it.

He popped to the surface and took in long, shuddering breaths, scanning the sky to find no sign of the jet. A familiar slapping noise came dully through his water-filled ears. He pushed at the ocean until he turned around and brought the rubber raft into view.

A grizzled SEAL bent down from the raft and gave him a hand up, asking with a grin, "You ever see one of them jarhead Marines look so good?"

"Never saw one look better," Bolan replied truthfully as he took the man's hand.

Gold Eagle launches an
exciting new Vietnam series.

HATCHET

Knox Gordon

Aerial Intel indicates a major buildup in the
Parrot's Beak region of Cambodia—long a
staging area into South Vietnam. Ordered to
recon the area, the hard-hitting Hatchet team
hits the field, testing their true abilities as
jungle fighters against an enemy who has
nothing to lose.

In the air and on the ground, behind the desks
and in the jungles...the action-packed new
series of the Vietnam War.

GOLD EAGLE

**The Eagle now lands at different times
at your retail outlet!**

Be sure to look for your favorite action adventure from Gold
Eagle on these dates each month.

Publication Month	In-Store Dates
September	August 21
October	September 25
November	October 23
December	November 20

We hope that this new schedule will be convenient for you.

Please note: There may be slight variations in on-sale dates
in your area due to differences in shipping and handling.

GEDATES-1

The Guardian Strikes

David North

A cloud of deadly gas is about to settle, and then a madman's dreams for a perfect society will be fulfilled. Behind it all is a sinister being searching for life-giving energy. He is the last of an ancient godlike race called the Guardians, and his survival hinges on the annihilation of the Earth's population.

Standing between him and survival are two men—the former CIA counterinsurgency specialist and the swordsman from the mists of time. Once again they join forces across time to defeat the savage being determined to destroy both their worlds.

Look for THE GUARDIAN STRIKES, Book 3 of the Gold Eagle miniseries TIME WARRIORS.

Bolan is no stranger to the hellfire trail.

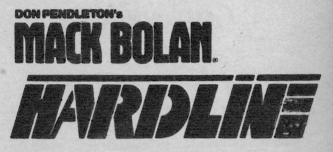

DON PENDLETON's
MACK BOLAN.

HARDLINE

Corrupt electronics tycoons are out to make a killing by selling ultrasecret military hardware to anyone with the cash. One of their targets is a man with one foot in the grave, an occult-obsessed defense contractor.

Mack Bolan finds himself enmeshed in a mission that grows more bizarre by the minute, involving spirits and Stealth, mystics and murderers.